TALES
FROM THE
OUTPOST

VOLUME ONE

F.X. MANDICH

Excerpt from: Tales From The Outpost, Volume Two ©2016 by F.X. Mandich.

First Edition: June, 2016

ISBN-10: 0-9976248-0-9

ISBN-13: 978-0-9976248-0-9

Printed in the United States of America

DEDICATION

For my friend, Beth Bonner –

You were not with us long enough...

CONTENTS

ACKNOWLEDGEMENTS

For Al, my husband: You don't always understand me, but I think that's a good thing! I do love you!

For my daughters, Elisabeth and Gina: My biggest fans...You've given me so much happiness and I'm so very proud of the women and mothers you have become. I love you fiercely!

For Jake, Madison, Ava, Olivia, Ethan, Arty, Jessica, Vanessa, Lauren, Emily, Robert, Natalie, Annabela and Sophia: I love you all!

For Daniel and Jonathan: I am honored to have been a part of your lives and watching you grow into such wonderful men. I love you both!

For my Friends who've been with me forever: Thank you for your love and support. My love is with you.

Special thanks goes to Elisabeth for her great patience in the editing of this volume

Thank you...all of you.

ESTATE SALE

<u>PART ONE</u>

John and Julia McKenna climbed into their Volvo sedan and John started up the engine.

"Jul, I'm telling you, I think that piece is worth money. Not a fortune maybe, but certainly a great deal more than the seventy-five bucks you just paid for it."

Julia smiled smugly. She knew the minute she saw the small piece that it was a Royal Doulton inspired by Renoir. As she was walking through the library room of the outsized Victorian house, she'd noticed that a large woman had zeroed in on it at almost the same time, but Julia had startled her into turning around by issuing a small but noisy intake of breath as if she had seen a mouse or other impertinent creature on one the bookshelves behind the woman.

She then sped past her and laid hands upon the statuette. The woman eyed her menacingly, but Julia had hold of it and that was that! She even managed to bargain her way from the one-hundred-dollar asking price down to seventy-five dollars. Well, she reasoned, if people were selling off their relatives' old possessions, they should be smart enough to have a professional go through the house first. They would do well to spend a few dollars of their own and have things appraised, just in case something valuable should be hidden amongst the old linens and lamps and dishes and other paraphernalia that people tended to collect in a lifetime of living.

However, it was better for her that they generally did not go through this trouble. Since his retirement, she and John had been going to "estate sales" and then re-selling the pieces they'd discovered. They'd actually made more money than they did from John's pension, and he had worked twenty-five years at a job that was barely tolerable to him in order to be eligible for that meager monthly stipend. Now, they got to tour all over the countryside just looking for these sales and their next big buy.

It had all started quite by accident really, on a Friday evening shortly after John retired, almost three years ago. Julia was sitting in the living room of their cozy, single family home in Ridgewood, finishing up a quilt that she was making for their sixth grandchild.

She looked...contented, John thought, and very much like the girl he'd married so long ago – not at all like a grandma. He grinned and when she looked up questioningly, he simply shook his head. Julia shrugged and went back to her sewing.

She planned to give the quilt to Ethan along with the matching pillow sham as a Christmas gift. Her daughter had told her that Ethan was going to be sleeping in his own bed by January because he was a "big boy" now, according to him, and Julia wanted him to have something special. Besides, with five other grandchildren on their gift list, the quilt was the most economical way to go and still have a present that would be exceptional. She had found herself making more and more gifts lately...for their grandchildren, for her three sisters and their grandchildren and for any special events that came up, such as weddings and showers and christenings.

Their obligations had grown and John's pension and their social security allowance were not keeping up with their burgeoning list. Using their paltry savings for such frivolities was not even an option. God forbid the furnace went or their car needed work done...they had to have some kind of cushion to fall back upon. Their daughters Jacqueline and JoAnn had both offered to help, and were generous in their gift-giving with their parents, sending them on cruises and vacations almost every year. Each had married fine men and, while not rich, could well afford to subsidize their parents. However, neither John nor Julia would hear of it; vacations were one thing – handouts, another! They did not want to become a financial burden to their children. Not ever!

So, on this particular Friday, John had suggested that they go for a ride up north the next day and pick apples...maybe even buy some cider to mull on a chilly evening. Julia thought it would be a wonderful idea.

"We can pack a picnic lunch and make a day of it. How does some fried chicken sound?"

"Sounds as good as it did forty-two years ago," John said. He shook his head wryly and sighed. "We didn't have much money then either, remember? Funny, I didn't think we'd still be rowing that same boat now. Oh well, some things just never change."

Julia nuzzled her husband's cheek as he came up behind her and gave her a bear hug. Oh, but she did love him. They'd met while he was a senior in high school and she was a sophomore. He was tall, dark and very serious looking until he flashed his lopsided grin. Once he flashed it her way, she was smitten. She was afraid he would never really be interested in her though. At fifteen, Julia Baker was short - only five-foot-three, and a bit overweight. On the positive side, however, she had clear ivory skin and wide emerald green eyes. These, she felt, were her only advantages. She failed to realize that patience, intelligence, kindness and a genial disposition were the plusses that attracted people to her. They didn't fail to attract John. They started going steady two months after they met.

When they'd married after college, he'd had so many dreams...he'd wanted to write the great American novel and had actually been able to publish a short story in a magazine once. But...that once had been all there ever was. He'd work the nine to five grind during the day and hurry off to his typewriter right after dinner almost every night. Julia had encouraged him for a while, but over time had lost heart. She'd never discouraged him exactly; she loved him too much for that. She had simply begun to lose her great store of patience and quietly carp - to her mother, to her mother-in-law, to her two sisters - about having to pick up on his chores as well as having to raise the kids, clean the house, do the laundry, shop for food, cook, iron, ad infinitum. And it *was* justified. Not only did she have all the household chores, but she was working as well. She got out her old portable and typed lawyer's briefs four hours every day while her husband was at work and while the kids were in school. She worked from home to make a bit of additional money for small family vacations and the like. By the end of a typical day, she found herself totally exhausted, and she felt she was sniping at the kids once too often lately. After all, how far could she be expected to stretch herself in a twenty-four-hour period?

John never made a conscious decision to stop writing. He just did it less and less until his old Smith-

Corona sat forlornly in a corner of the den gathering dust. He had begun to notice Julia's shortness of patience with the kids too. Resigned, he simply went to work every day at the office and hated it more and more. He never begrudged his family though. He knew what he had to do and in his life, his family came first. Julia had made a wonderful home for him and their two daughters. If working this job was the small sacrifice he had to make for all of them, then so be it. Dreaming was for children and people without any responsibilities anyway. It was not for him.

That weekend of apple picking had changed their lives forever.

They had randomly chosen a road and began driving, finding themselves meandering through a beautiful, wooded area of Connecticut. It was a perfect Indian summer day. The air was clean and crisp and the sun shone warm and bright. They found themselves relaxed and care-free for the first time in a long time.

"Hey, sweetie. I'm hungry. What about you?" John asked.

Julia agreed. "Next place, we'll stop. Maybe we can find a small park or something."

As they drove, they discovered something even better and pulled over to a small farm stand where apples and everything made of apples abounded.

"Oh, it smells delicious." Julia commented. "Hey, there's picnic tables out back. What say we have our picnic lunch here?"

John took their basket from the back of the SUV and they headed for a table under the trees in back.

The menu seemed to overflow with all things apple – cider, pies, cakes, sauce, muffins and even apple pancakes. The delicious smell of apples and cinnamon hung heavily in the air, mingling with the fragrance of a fire burning merrily in the old wood stove in a corner.

They stood on line at the counter and Julia ordered for them both, choosing hot, mulled apple ciders.

"With caramel sauce and two cinnamon apple muffins!" John interjected.

"Oh, let us not forget your sweet-tooth!" Julia snickered good-naturedly.

"Hey!" John laughed.

They settled in at their table, setting it with the picnic-ware they had brought in their basket. Looking around them, they marveled at the beautiful foliage. Yellows, oranges and russets of many hues vied for attention with each other. The huge evergreens behind them made a perfect foil for their splendor.

"I think, Jul, that sometimes we forget the really good things that we can have without a lot of money," John remarked quietly as he gazed at their surroundings.

"You're right, John. But sometimes the 'have-nots' are just so damned imposing."

They started on their lunch then and settled into the comfortable silence that intimacy allows.

A well-dressed, middle-aged couple approached, holding hands and laughing together. Julia could not help but notice the huge diamond the woman wore above her wedding ring as it flashed in the sun. They seated themselves at an adjacent table after ordering at the counter. They talked animatedly as they unwrapped their fare and ate in silence. Then the woman spoke.

"Can you believe the price on that vintage Judith Leiber? And it was in mint condition. It looked as if it had never been outside of its velvet bag. They had no clue how much it was worth. I almost felt bad…the key word here being 'almost'." She flashed a dazzling smile at her companion and sipped at her hot apple cider.

"They usually don't," he replied returning her smile. "But what the hey…it's still a win/win situation. They're happy because they made a few bucks on their old man's 'junk' and we know what Victor will probably give us for it. I would estimate about two grand clear profit…and that's not such a bad day's wages, is it babe?"

"I thought about twenty-five hundred actually," she said.

"You know, you could be right," he answered. "But I'd say a minimum two thousand. There's so much fine detail work to consider, and top-of-the-line quality materials. And see, you didn't even want to go. You've told me a thousand times that you can't tell from the way the house looks what these people have. Even the most modest looking one can hold a treasure. Half the time, the original owner doesn't even know what they've got. They inherit it or get it as a gift and then toss it in the attic. A few years later they forget about it. And remember, most people don't know names. They wouldn't know a…" the man shook his head slowly as he searched his mind. "a Monet from a Picasso if they looked right at it. Hey…I don't feel guilty. So much the better for us if they don't. This isn't the worst way to make a living, Millie."

"Here's to those in the know!" The woman raised her glass of cider in salute and tipped her glass to his. "Here's to estate sales…and of course, to us. Always to us."

"Mmm…this is good stuff, isn't it Mil? C'mon though. Gotta go. It'll take us a good half-hour to get to the next one. Are you ready, hon?"

"Ready as I'll ever be," she answered as she picked up her handbag, throwing their leftovers into the bin.

Julia turned to find John staring in her direction, mouth halted in mid-chew. She had been in the same position herself and now managed to get her piece of chicken down her dry throat by gulping down a swallow of apple cider. Both the chicken and the cider had suddenly lost their taste.

"John...you heard what I heard, didn't you? I mean the part about two thousand dollars?"

John nodded in assent

"Do you think it's true?"

John nodded slowly. His bench was positioned in such a way that he had a complete view of the few picnic tables and the parking area. He tipped his chin in the direction behind Julia.

"Look," he said.

The couple were making their way towards their car. What looked like a relatively new silver gray Jaguar chirruped as the man stretched out his arm holding a remote entry device.

Julia turned, discretion forgotten and stared openly as the couple strolled towards the car and got in. The car's powerful engine was barely audible as they pulled away.

"Estate sale?" Julia queried when she finally turned back to John.

"Estate sale." John confirmed.

And that had been the beginning.

Now it was what the McKenna's lived for…and on.

When they got home that evening, they sat up until very late drinking cup after cup of rich coffee and eating thin slices of the fresh baked apple pie they had bought that afternoon. All the while they talked about the possibilities of making some kind of extra cash from these estate sales.

"After all," John said, "the only investment we need make is in gas for the car. We can get all the information we need about antiques and buying and prices by going to the library and researching, and then there's the internet. And I have no trouble believing people have things lying around that they don't know are worth good money – *especially* when things are inherited from relatives. Remember two years ago when you went to that garage sale and found those two ceramic cocker spaniels? You just thought they were cute because they reminded you of Misty and then your sister came over and told you that she saw the very same ones in that antique shop in Red Bank for fifty dollars for the pair. And what did you pay? Fifty cents, right?

"What were they...uh...Global or something? I know they were 'vintage.' All the way from 1972." John chuckled. "For some reason, 1972 doesn't sound so 'vintage' to me!"

"You're right about the year, but it was 'Goebel' John." Julia giggled. "Not 'Global' you goose!"

"Whatever," John said.

"And, I'd forgotten about those, but you're right. I guess people do have treasures they don't know about, but we'd need to know an awful lot, John."

"So, like I said, we research. We have that computer that Mark gave us. We can hook up to the internet...He said that you can find out about tons of stuff that way. Between the computer and the library, we should be set to go. What do you say, Jul? Think about it. What do we have to lose? It could be the beginning of a new life for us."

"Oh, John, it almost scares me to even consider not scrimping anymore. Just think, we could take the kids on vacation for once and get some real gifts for everyone and…and the kids won't have to worry about us anymore. Do you think we really could do this?"

"Yes," he said. "I think we really could."

# # #

That Monday, they went downtown to the library and started researching everything they could on antique furniture, glass, pottery and artwork. It was much more of an undertaking than they had imagined. There were literally thousands of books available, and the information on the internet was mind-boggling. They basically spent the next several weeks absorbing all they could, spending four or five hours a day in the cavernous library, and on the library's computers. After a quick lunch, they'd visit antique shops where they would be able to view pieces firsthand and speak to the owners or anyone else willing to provide them with answers to their questions.

Finally, one weekend, armed with their new knowledge, they checked out their newspaper on a Thursday night, marking off the estate sales in the local area.

They found three.

The first sale they went to was in Huntington. The newspaper said the sale would be from nine a.m. to four p.m. They arrived at nine-fifteen and ended up cruising around another fifteen minutes looking for a parking space. When they finally squeezed themselves through the front door, they found the house packed with people.

"Oh, my goodness!" Julia said. "This place is mobbed!"

A lissome, blonde woman standing next to Julia who had apparently overheard, turned to her and smiled.

"Sure it is," she said. "Almost everyone here is a dealer. We've been here since eight o'clock this morning, waiting outside to get in. This place was owned by someone who was an avid collector, so it's a bit more crowded than it usually is. I guess you're new to the game?"

"Yes." John said. "It's our first time. We've just come to kind of check it out and see what there is."

"A lot of people do that," the woman said. "Sometimes there are great things around that no one has noticed that are worth a small fortune. Sometimes, people list it as an estate sale and they're just getting rid of old junk. You never know. But, you've gotta get here early or else everything's been picked over by the pros."

"I see," John said. "I assume you're one of the pros?"

"Guilty as charged!" the woman answered smiling broadly. "My name is Anke. Anke Garamond. I have a small antique shop in Manhattan. I spend my weekends traveling around looking for eclectic pieces."

She dug into her purse and came out with a small card.

"Here's my card. If you ever find something that looks good, bring it in. I can probably tell you what it's worth right off and if you're interested in selling, maybe we can strike a deal. If it's something

I can't use, I might be able to put you in touch with someone who's interested in it."

"Hey, thanks. Thanks a lot, Anke. My name's John McKenna and this is my wife, Julia."

As the crowd progressed from room to room, the three chatted amiably.   She was very willing to share her vast wealth of knowledge with them and pointed out pieces of interest and what the two should watch out for when they were on their own.

"There are so many reproductions out there, and some of them are really good…they could fool even the 'experts' like me," Anke told them. "You just have to arm yourself with as much knowledge as possible to avoid being taken. But, be prepared. Like I said, it happens to the best of us."

An hour-and-a-half later, the three parted company on the front steps of the large house. Julia and John both felt as if they'd made a friend in the business who could give them a few pointers when necessary and even provide them with an outlet for their purchases. All in all, it had been a fruitful morning.

They went to two other sales that afternoon, and actually found a first edition Hemmingway that was touted as having been signed by the author. Neither Julia nor John knew enough about signatures to know if it was truly Hemmingway's signature or not and so decided to pass on it.

Driving home that night, they were very quiet. Each felt a tinge of disappointment at not having found anything exciting, and along with that came apprehension...were they headed down a path of folly? They both began speaking at the same time.

"Do you think we're doing the right thing?" they voiced.

The moment broke the tension. Both started laughing.

John spoke first.

"Yes, Jul. I think we're doing the right thing. Don't you?"

"Yes. I believe I actually do. I think..." she hesitated, tried to find the right words. "I think that we almost *need* to do this...for us. We've got to try. Not just for the money, even though that's an important issue, but for us."

"Yeah, I think I know what you mean, Jul. It's just you and me now and we're in another phase of our life. I can't see that phase playing out as two people sitting alone in the house every night; me with the boob-tube going and you sitting in the wing chair crocheting or knitting or quilting until your fingers are bleeding, each of us waiting for the end.

"We need to have an 'adventure.' Something to make our lives fun again and interesting and…and…worth living. You know what I mean? I don't want to just '*be*'!

"You remember that old song Jul…'I'm Gonna Live Till I Die'? *That's* how I feel!"

Julia smiled at her husband's impassioned speech. He was right though. They might have to take a few chances, perhaps make a few mistakes, but it was better than becoming one of the walking dead.

She did not know how that thought would come back to haunt her in the very near future.

The following Thursday they found four estate sales in the area. There were three on Friday and one on Saturday. They plotted their course on a map so that they would waste neither gas nor time. Thursday night they went to bed early having planned to be at the first sale by eight-thirty in the morning. This time, they would be a bit better prepared.

They got back home late Friday afternoon, weary from all the walking they'd done. They'd arrived at the first house with time to spare, but found to their dismay that the house had practically been picked clean.

"Oh, we have a friend who's an antiques dealer," the woman sitting by the front door explained. "He was here yesterday morning with his truck. We didn't think he was going to take so much of our mother's things, but, he did!" she finished brightly.

"Do you think the Fates are trying to tell us something?" Julia asked as they turned and left.

"Yup, I do," John replied without hesitation. "I think they're trying to tell us to wear a good pair of shoes when we go out on these expeditions, because we're gonna be doin' a hellava lot of walking!"

Julia laughed delightedly. She was so happy that John was taking this with such equanimity.

By the time they reached the third house, however, she wasn't so sure about either John's or her own ability to look at the bright side.

House number two had been a bust. It was in a home on a hill overlooking Long Island Sound. They both looked at each other with apprehension when they drove up and saw what it looked like. "Mansion" was the word that came into both their minds. Everything was being auctioned off, including the contents of the huge greenhouse which sat at an angle to the south of the house. Julia was tempted to purchase an exotic orchid, but the temptation only lasted until she heard the bidding begin on another orchid very similar to the one she was holding. There was no way she was paying over ninety dollars for a flower – rare or not! And, that was one of the least expensive things being auctioned off.

House number three wasn't much better. The house was much smaller by far than number two, but the prices were still astronomical. By speaking to a few people there, they discovered the reason.

The home had belonged to Senator Harrison F. Richards, who had just recently passed away. So, it seemed that even though the items themselves were not truly worth the small fortune listed, the fact that they had belonged to a famous Senator added at least an extra zero to the price-tag.

"It's all right, Jul," John said. "It's only a matter of time. Rome wasn't built in a day."

"Well, Rome didn't have a stack of bills waiting to be paid either," Julia snapped, instantly wishing she hadn't. "I'm sorry, hon. I'm just tired and anxious. I'll get past it, don't worry."

John didn't answer.

Saturday's sale was in Mount Sinai. It was a long ride from Ridgewood, but the weather forecast called for a sunny day so they packed a picnic lunch. They arrived at fifty-nine Apple Lane at eight-thirty in the morning and pulled up in front of the elegant old stone structure. The house stood by itself atop a gentle incline, surrounded by graceful sycamore trees. It was the only one on the block. There were no other cars visible, save for a beautifully maintained nineteen-forty Packard parked at the top of the driveway.

"I don't know if this is a good sign or a bad one," Julia commented.

"What," John said. "That no one has arrived yet?"

"Yes," Julia answered. "If no one's here by nine, what should we do? Just go up and ring the doorbell?"

"I guess so, Jul. They advertised the sale. Someone will be around, I'm sure."

As it turned out, by nine o'clock, no one had shown up. However, an elderly man wearing a hounds-tooth porkpie hat had come out from inside the house and was scrupulously cleaning the windshield of the old Packard.

John and Julia walked together up the driveway and approached the man, who looked up and smiled as they came near.

"Hello. Are you here for the sale?"

"Yes, we are," John said. "Were we incorrect about the time or the date? It seems we're the only ones around."

"Oh, no, no," the man assured them. "You're right on target.   There are a few people here, but they've all come in through the main entrance. It's on the other side…Apple Lane sort of wraps around you see."

"Oh," Julia said. "We didn't realize that this wasn't it.   Would it be all right if we just walked around the outside to get into the house?"

"I should think so," the man said. "If you go around here to your left, you can cut through the courtyard. Just go straight across it and look to your right and you'll see the main entrance. I'm quite certain it will be busy enough by now."

"Thanks." John said.

They started walking and found the courtyard easily enough and realized that the part of the house that they could see from where they were parked was only the tip of the iceberg, so to speak.

"Wow," John said, looking around.

An enormous three tier fountain stood at the center of the cobblestone courtyard.   A lovely, wrought-iron archway, at least twenty-feet in width, emblazoned with the initial "B" marked its main entrance, while two other smaller archways could be seen from where Julia and John had entered. To their immediate left stood a garage with no less than six doors.

"Wow," John repeated.

"Yes..." Julia said slowly. "You know, if we couldn't afford anything at that other place, what do you think is going to happen here?"

"Well, look at it this way, Jul. We can have fun just browsing around inside of a place we would never have gotten to see otherwise."

Julia looked at her husband sideways. He was becoming quite the little optimist of late, she noticed. If all this poking around at estate sales ever did was lift his spirits, then they would have benefited tremendously, she thought.

The whole house had been opened up for the sale, including the attic on the third floor. Everything, no matter how trivial, had been meticulously marked with the asking price. Apparently everything in the house was being sold, up to and including family portraits. As they wandered through the rooms, they noticed the elderly man they had seen outside in the back of the house. He greeted them genially, telling them his name was Hank, and they exchanged small talk as they walked. He then proceeded to tell them that the house had been owned by a very elderly woman who'd only recently passed away, leaving everything to her servants and her three dogs. Hank had been her chauffeur and in conjunction with the gardener, the housekeeper and the woman's personal maid, had decided to sell everything they did not want personally, take the money and retire. The gardener, he said, was taking the three dogs.

"I've had enough of driving other people's cars to where they want to go," he said. "It's time I drive myself around now."

He walked with them through a few of the rooms, showing them around and then he took a small object from a table that was tucked behind a large potted plant.

It was a small, pale green figurine.

"The mum's grandfather brought it back from Tunisia where he was visiting with some old friends. He thinks they got it on the black market. It's a

Chinese relic and probably shouldn't even have left the country but...they could get away with a lot more in those days...officials could be bribed much more easily and openly then, you know."

John and Julia smiled politely at Hank and exchanged puzzled glances with each other.

"You seem like nice people," he said. "Mrs. Barrymore was a generous employer. A good sort. She always believed that good deeds would always come back to you. She did a good deed for us by leaving us this house. The truth be told, she really didn't have any other relatives, but she still didn't have to leave it to us. I've come to believe in her philosophy...what goes around comes around and all that. Here. I want you to have this." He thrust the small figurine towards Julia.

"We couldn't," Julia protested immediately.

"Sure you could," the man said. "See? There's not even a price on it. That's because I put it on the side for myself. If you don't take it, I'll just have to walk around half the day, looking for someone else I take a fancy to who would like to have it. Please. It would make me feel good to do this."

They thanked him and then walked around the house for almost an hour with Hank as their tour guide. As it turned out, Julia had been right. Anything that looked interesting or that had possibilities, they could not afford. John did find a beautifully bound book on antiquities, however, and gladly paid the forty-seven dollar asking price for it. They left after thanking Hank again for his generosity.

"What do you think, Jul?" John asked after they'd gotten back into their car.

"I think it was a lovely gesture," Julia said.

"No, no," John said. "I mean, do you think it's worth anything?"

"John!" Julia exclaimed. "That's so…so…"

"Practical?" John offered. "Look, Jul. I hate to come up empty again this weekend."

"You are too much," she said grinning.

They took the figurine to Anke the following Monday. She examined it closely.

"It's jade all right," she said. "It's in beautiful condition. I'll have to check my book to see if I can get an idea of its approximate value. Can you wait a few minutes?"

A half-hour later, Anke emerged from behind the book she had been studying. The book itself was the size of four phone books placed in a square and was about six inches thick.

"That's some book," John remarked as she closed it with a thud.

"I don't think there's another one like it in existence. It's the 'Lineage of Antiquities' by Cornelius Welheimer, translated from the German. I got it from my great aunt Maude. She was really into ancient pottery and religious artifacts and seventeenth century furniture." Anke told him. "And it's the best source of information on really old pieces I have."

"So you think this piece is really old?" Julia questioned.

"Mmm, yes…In my opinion, I would say that it's really, really old," Anke confirmed. "It actually looks like a Dushan jade ornament. They were unearthed from the tombs of Shang kings, but that would make the value…incalculable. It would be from the Shang Dynasty, you see, and that would make this piece almost three thousand years old."

Julia gasped.

"I can't find one with exactly the same carvings as this one, but I would say it's comparable to the ones in here. Sometimes that's as close as we can get. The thing of it is, you see, that if it's really from that Dynasty, I don't know if it could even be sold – except perhaps, to a private collector. The Chinese government would be all over it otherwise. The other thing is, it might be a replica – still quite old and quite valuable though. Of course, it would have to be authenticated by a competent authority to tell us which of the two it is. An authority that is, other than myself. I only have so much expertise and in this case, that's not quite enough I'm afraid."

Anke looked at them intently. "Unofficially, I would say, you have a piece that's possibly worth hundreds of thousands of dollars – maybe a lot more. You could have something here worth a small fortune…something you could retire on."

"You're sure?" Julia asked, almost in a whisper.

"Well, as I said, being officially unofficial…yes. And, if you'd like, I can put you in contact with the people who *can* officially authenticate it. They'll give you the documents on it so that when you find a collector, you'll be set to go. Not to burst your bubble on this Julia, but I almost hope it's a replica. If it's for real, it's going to be a hassle to sell it, and if the Chinese get wind, I don't know what recourse you will have. It could be that it's a stolen antiquity, and all that will get you is aggravation. It will cost you to have an authentication done though…roughly two to three hundred dollars, but I'll talk to Myron Retski – he's the person I had in mind, and he'll be fair."

John and Julia left the city totally elated. They couldn't believe all that had happened that day. Possibly garnering more than John's lifetime pension in a matter of hours was incredible. They each secretly calculated what they could do with this kind of money if they could make even a tenth of that once a month or even once every other month…Of course, if it wasn't a replica, they could retire now with never another care in the world. True, money cannot buy happiness, Julia reminded herself, but on the other hand, it could certainly keep a lot of *un*happiness at bay!

<u>PART TWO</u>

"Jul! Jul! Hey there! What happened? Fall asleep?"

Julia blinked rapidly, trying to shake the grogginess off.

"Mmm…I guess I did," she admitted. "All of a sudden, I just got so tired…I wonder whatever happened to Hank…"

John didn't even have to ask who Julia was talking about. After they'd sold that jade piece (it turned out that it was a replica, but still worth more than John's pension for the next five years) they tried to call him – they'd even driven out to Mount Sinai and gone to Fifty-nine Apple in search of him, but the house had been boarded up and the gates locked. When they'd gotten back home that night, they drank a toast to Hank with a bottle of Dom wishing him a long and happy retirement.

"I guess it was good that the ornament was just a replica. If it had been the real thing, we could have been out the authentication money and had nothing to show for it if the Chinese government got wind of it. Well, I hope Hank is at least as happy as we are," John said. He smiled, looking across the seat at his wife.

He still found her so terribly appealing when she was just awakening from sleep. She always looked so very young and vulnerable…just as she had when they'd first met. He'd never voiced his feeling to her, but that was what had attracted him to her…that quality of vulnerability. Actually, he never dared voice it to her – given the fact that in the sixties, women were burning bras and declaring their right to be the equal of men in almost every facet of life. Vulnerability, he felt, might not be a trait she would appreciate him revering. He thought, however, that one day in the not-too-distant future, he might just tell her about this engaging quality of hers and see what she thought about it.

They went straight to the city to see Anke with their latest discovery and then the three went for dinner at Aqua Vite in Manhattan. They left after dropping Anke off at her East Side apartment, having declined to stay for an after-dinner aperitif. They wanted to get home early they told her because they had three sales slated for tomorrow…one in Tarrytown, one on Long Island and one in Queens. The driving alone was going to be a killer.

# # #

The day started off on a high note. They'd decided to make their first stop in Forest Hills. This particular part of Queens was still considered an up-market neighborhood, but the exterior of the graceful Victorian house they were heading into was in the first stages of deterioration. Not true of the interior, however. It looked as if time had stood still within its walls. It had been owned by a ninety-five-year-old spinster who had been born in one of the upstairs bedrooms. She took care of her parents until their deaths some thirty years ago and had remained in her house, essentially never changing anything from the way her parents had left it. Chandeliers, paintings, old family photographs in heavy silver frames – all had remained untouched. The velvet draperies had barred most of the sunlight so that even the carpets and the furnishings were in excellent condition. It was a buyer's paradise!

John and Julia headed upstairs, opting to check out the bedrooms first. The first bedroom seemed to be a child's. It was filled with stuffed animals, dolls, old fashioned prams and baby cribs. Julia's face softened as her eyes fell upon a doll with a porcelain face.

"I remember my grandmother had one of these. I named her Sara Darling. The 'Sara' was after my grandmother. Sometimes, when I was lonely or scared, I'd talk to Sara. She was a very good listener," Julia confided to John in a hushed tone. "And this doll is in wonderful condition. She even kind of reminds me of Sara, except that Sara was a blonde."

Julia held the beautiful doll at arm's length, admiring her. She wore a lavender colored silk dress decorated with delicate white flowers. The dress was partially hidden by a white, lace-trimmed pinafore. Ankle-high white leather boots in surprisingly pristine condition completed her outfit. Her dark brown curly hair framed a perfect angelic face with rosy, pink lips, tiny pearl-white teeth and huge blue eyes surrounded by black curled lashes. Julia caressed the doll's face tenderly and then replaced her on the child-size wicker chair.

"Why don't you check out what's in the other bedroom Jul while I finish checking out this one?" John offered. "This way we can save some time and get to the other sales earlier."

Julia agreed and wandered down the hall towards the back of the house. She found a three dimensional Victorian scene intricately carved out of alabaster. It was in an oval wood frame that had been painted a burnished gold and protected by an oval "bubble" of glass. She picked it up and turned it over, noting the aging brown paper that covered the back. She called John to come in and take a look at her find. When he didn't answer her call, she went back into the child's bedroom to look for him. He wasn't there.

Twenty minutes later, Julia had finished checking out the rest of the rooms, purchased the alabaster piece and went back to the car. She found John leaning casually against its side. The two always had a standing agreement to meet at their car when each was through so they would not waste precious time searching unfamiliar rooms for each other.

"I looked for you," Julia began.

"Well, I was waiting for you, right here." John said grinning broadly. "I found something…something I couldn't pass on."

John stepped aside.

Perched on the passenger seat of their car was the porcelain doll.

"Oh John, you didn't…"

"Yup, I did. You seemed so taken with her that I just couldn't pass her up. Besides, I thought she'd look nice in that empty corner near the fireplace. What do you think? Oh…and her chair is in the trunk."

Julia reached up on tiptoe and threw her arms around her husband's neck and kissed him squarely on the mouth, lingering there for a few moments. He returned her embrace and her kiss eagerly.

"I love you John McKenna," she said.

"I love you right back," he answered.

Their trip to Huntington proved to be fruitless. They moved through the house efficiently and were back in their car within a half-hour heading up to Tarrytown. Traffic, however, proved to be very uncooperative, and each road they took seemed to be worse than the last. Three hours later, they were at last moving through the Village of Tarrytown. By this time, John was insisting that they stop somewhere to eat. They had eaten nothing save for a small bowl of cereal that morning and even though she would not admit it, John knew that Julia would be feeling light-headed by now.

As they drove up Broad Street, they spotted a small luncheonette, "Main Street Caboose" and pulled into a parking space right in front.

"Sara will be safe in here, yes?" Julia said to John. "I really don't want to put her in the trunk."

"Sara?" John queried, eyebrows raised.

"Yes, Sara. I named her after my other Sara."

"Whatever makes you happy, hon. And yes, to answer your question. She'll be safe. The back windows are darker than the front, Jul. I doubt if anyone will even see her sitting back there."

Mollified, Julia trailed behind John who held the door open for his wife to enter. They slipped into a booth for two towards the front and both ordered grilled cheese sandwiches, a side salad and a diet soda. They were presented with their salads within minutes and both ate hungrily.

Julia put her fork down and sat back when she was through.

"Wow! I didn't realize how hungry I was. Good thing we stopped, but I hope the sandwiches are out quickly. We don't have much time left before it's dark. I just can't believe that traffic was sooo bad. I don't know if it even pays to go at this point. It's so late…everything has been picked over by now and I'm sure, all the good stuff is long gone."

"Mmm," John replied, pushing his empty salad plate to the side. He carefully wiped his mouth with his napkin before going on. "Well hon, look at the bright side. Perhaps all the junk is being removed before we get there, and we'll be left with just the good stuff."

"OK, John. And did I tell you about this bridge that's for sale…?" Julia teased.

John grinned and their sandwiches arrived.

They ate quickly and paid their bill at the cashier's counter up front.

"Everything all right folks?" the cashier asked.

"Oh, yes...just fine," John replied, taking his change and shoving it in his jacket pocket. "By the way, do you think you could tell us where number six-sixty-six Hemlock Hill is? It's supposed to be off..."

"Center Street," the man finished, head cocked inquisitively. "You're going there... now?"

"Yes." John replied.

As they followed the directions they had been given, Julia's brow was furrowed in concentration.

"Why do you think he was acting so...weird?" she asked her husband.

"You think he was weird?"

"Uh-huh. I do. He kind of...I don't know...got sort of strange after you gave him the address. Didn't you notice?"

"Not really," John said. "Maybe he just had something on his mind."

"Yeah...maybe..." Julia said, sounding unconvinced. "Oh, here's Center Street John. Make a right."

John dutifully followed his wife's directions and headed down Center, unaware that he was closing in on a nightmare.

PART THREE

"OK...this is...uh...strange..."

"Are you just finding everything 'weird and strange' today, Jul?"

"No. Just this."

They had made the left onto Hemlock Hill and followed its serpentine path as it wound slowly upward. There were no houses visible and the only streetlamp in sight was flashing on and off, intermittently throwing long and bizarre shadows on the street below.

"You know John, maybe we should just turn back. After all, it is kind of late..."

"Jul, the sale is going on 'till five according to the paper. It's only four-thirty now. And I'm not turning back until we at least see the place. We've been driving half the damned day and I'm not stopping now just 'cause you're getting the willies."

"Maybe we shouldn't have stopped to eat," Julia offered. "We might have saved more time that way."

"Sure we would have. We would have saved a whole twenty minutes or so, but it would still be dark or pretty darn close to it. And, my dear girl, you would have been complaining that you were light-headed or nauseated or some such thing."

"Hey, don't snipe at me. I didn't want to stop, remember? I could have lived with the light-headed thing for a few more minutes. Besides, I just don't like this. I don't know. It just gives me the creeps."

"Jul, be sensible. We're just in a quiet, suburban area. We've been in neighborhoods like this before."

"I agree, John. However, this is almost nighttime and it's…creepy."

John heaved an exasperated sigh.

"Jul, I love ya, but sometimes you make me crazy."

"That's my job, hon. If I didn't do it, who would?"

John chuckled. Then he spotted the large silhouette of a house against the darkening sky ahead.

"Hey! Maybe this is it," he said peering into the darkness. He slowed the car and turned so that its headlights illuminated the front. "Yup. There's the house number: six sixty-six."

As they pulled into the dirt driveway, they could see lights that seemed to be coming from the back of the house.

"Strange again," Julia commented as she stepped out from the car.

"Again?" John said.

"Well, don't you find it odd that there's no light at all in front of the house? I mean, if you're having an estate sale, wouldn't you light up the house so people could find it easier? Besides, how come no light is penetrating the front? When we put on even just our kitchen lights in the back of the house, you can still see some sort of lambent light coming through the front windows."

"Jul, how would I know? Maybe they have heavy draperies in the front and the light doesn't penetrate…or maybe the front is separated by doors and they have them all closed so no light is coming through. Maybe they didn't open up the whole house for the sale. Maybe they only opened up the back rooms and maybe someone didn't realize that in the dark the house is almost impossible to see and they simply forgot to turn on a light. Again, Jul, how should I know?"

John's exasperated tone made Julia stamp her foot in anger and frustration.

"John McKenna…sometimes I…I…"

"You what, Julia Baker?"

Julia couldn't help it. John's goofy lopsided grin and the use of her maiden name always stopped her anger mid-stream.

"I want a divorce!" she exclaimed trying not to laugh.

"Sure! As soon as we get home," he replied amiably.

John held out his hand for his wife to grasp as they ventured through the dark path to the front of the old dwelling.

Julia knew it was ludicrous, but she had goose-bumps nevertheless. Something wasn't right here. She could feel it in her bones. She opened her mouth to say as much to her husband, but then snapped it shut again. I'm beginning to sound like a nervous old biddy, she thought as she looked up at her husband's strong profile. She needed John to take the reins on this one. She was working herself up into a full-blown panic and she knew it. Momentarily, she would content herself with being strong in their home life. He could take over here, thank you very much!

They could hear the big brass knocker resounding from within the house, but there was no sign of anyone coming to the door. They made their way to the back of the big house and John reached for the large glass doorknob.

"John, exactly why are we doing this? I really don't care if they have the original Mona Lisa hanging up in there, and they're selling it for a whopping ten dollars. I want to go home!"

"Come on, Jul. Why are you being so antsy?"

"I don't know. Atavistic reaction. I can't help it."

"Just come on. We're fine."

He pushed open the door then and was greeted by a scene of total familiarity.

Several people were walking around, chatting amongst themselves and checking out the price tags and labels on various items. John took Julia's hand and guided her through the large eat-in kitchen from where they had entered towards the front entrance. As they approached the large foyer, they noticed a woman sitting at a baby grand piano that was in an alcove to the left. She was playing Beethoven's Fifth Concerto, and doing so beautifully, from what Julia knew of the piece. The woman herself was extremely lovely, Julia noted, with a perfect profile, milky white skin and thick, coppery hair, plaited loosely in the back. Julia turned to her husband and noticed, with equanimity, that he was gazing, unabashedly, in the piano woman's direction. She poked him in the ribs with her elbow and he started.

"Having daydreams again, are we?" she asked, grinning up at him.

"Huh?"

"Earth to John…Earth to John…are you in there? And, by the way, don't you find it strange

(there's that word again, she thought)

that there are no cars anywhere outside, but this room is filled with people?"

John snapped to, all business.

Totally ignoring her question, he said, "Let's start by looking over there in that corner, Jul. That chest looks interesting."

"Hmm, OK," Julia said.

They found everything interesting, but nothing out of the ordinary. Slowly, they worked their way around the room until they neared the piano where the woman was still playing.

Now that they were closer, Julia noticed that the woman was not as stunning as she had thought when she first saw her. Her skin was etched with fine lines and her hair was not quite the shiny copper-red that it had first appeared to be. Her hands, Julia noticed with some surprise, were dotted with age spots. But the music was most definitely exceptional.

Glancing around again, she noticed an open jewelry box in what appeared to have been the dining room.

"John, I'm heading over to the other room for a minute to check out the jewelry, OK? Oh, and no meeting at the car this time, all right? You just stay...around here," Julia gestured loosely with her hand. "I'll meet you back here."

"Sure, sure, Jul. I'll just be browsing around in here."

Julia looked curiously at her husband, shrugged and then went inside.

John started moving away from the piano.

Julia made her way into the dining room and the open jewelry box.

John was walking away and then glanced down at the woman seated on the bench. Her eyes were the most startling shade of blue he'd ever seen, fringed by thick black lashes. He found them... compelling.

"You play beautifully, Ma'am. Beethoven, I believe?"

"He wrote beautifully and thank you. My name is Clarissa. Clarissa Montgomery. And you would be...?"

John hesitated. He was being drawn in by those beautiful eyes...and those lips...full and soft and pink like a rose petal. He swallowed hard.

"John. John McKenna. Are you the owner of this house, or are you contemplating purchasing this Steinway?"

"I am the owner, John. My husband, Roland, is gone and I find this house just too much for me." She lowered her head and when she looked back up at him, her eyes glistened with unshed tears. "My husband and I were never blessed with any children. And now, even with the servants, the house is...empty."

John found himself immensely saddened by her situation. His heart went out to her. He so wanted to comfort her…to lessen her pain…

"Have you found somewhere to go? I mean, a new home?"

"Yes, John. I have had a place waiting for me for awhile now."

"Where?" John asked.

(He *had* to know where she would be, what she would be doing…)

"Not too far from here really. I have grown so very fond of this area…of my friends and neighbors. I don't want to be too distanced from them all."

"Oh, of course. I understand," John agreed. "So tell me, have you lived here many years? Where are you from originally?"

Clarissa looked up at John and smiled.

"Come, John. Sit next to me and we will talk. I can tell you are an understanding man."

"Yes. Yes, I am," John agreed eagerly, sitting beside her.

As he sat, he noticed a faint, dank odor. Rather musty, he thought. Must be the old piano; perhaps the draperies hanging behind it. Those servants are probably not doing their job. Taking advantage of the poor woman's distraction. She needs someone to stand up for her in her time of need. Yes. She needs someone...

Julia held a costume brooch she'd discovered in the overflowing jewelry box. It bore no price tag as did most of the other pieces, but it looked quite old and was made of intricately worked "gold" encrusted with colored glass rubies, sapphires and a table-cut emerald at its center. She walked slowly around the large room, scrutinizing its contents. This room – this *house* – must have been so striking at one time she thought, surveying the wide crown molding and beautiful wainscoting. Besides the ornate mahogany table and chairs, there were antique paintings in heavy, gilded frames, oriental carpets and a huge cabinet filled with the most delicate china and crystal.

She was drawn to a particularly delicate teacup and saucer with a lovely, elaborate rose pattern. It was edged in gold – twenty-two-carat she thought – and she turned it over to see the maker's name. It was there, all right, but she couldn't read it distinctly. Realizing that she didn't have her reading glasses on, she put down the set and the brooch she'd been holding, and fished in her purse until she found her glasses. As she lifted her things from the table, her fingers brushed against the top of it and she noted the layer of dust; it was then that she noticed the dust that also covered the brooch and the tea set that she had just put down. She replaced them both very carefully on the table where the outline of the two items was very visible and untouched by the grime. She stood staring at the two pieces for a very long time, her heart hammering against her ribs although she was at a loss as to why. Julia imagined that it was terror that was clouding her vision, because when she looked up again, the room looked dimmer than it had before, and the lights were flickering.

John was enjoying himself immensely. He couldn't remember when he had had such a lively conversation with anyone. Clarissa was well-versed in music, in the arts and in literature. John found himself telling her about the book he had wanted to write so many years ago. He regaled her first with the broad outline, and when she expressed so much interest in his idea, he began to expound on the finer points. He told her honestly, that he had not considered an ending to this fine American drama, but he was sure that when he had it down on paper, the ending would present itself. Clarissa questioned him as to why he had stopped – why he had let his marvelous talent just sit for so many years. John told her, quite honestly he thought, that he'd had to make a choice between his career and his family and he had chosen to keep his family together. It was the "right thing to do, you see." Clarissa, meanwhile, had stopped playing and had turned her full attention to him. Her beautiful, incredible blue eyes misted over when he told her of the decision he had made.

"I'm sure you did what you had to do, John," she said in her soft voice. "I wish my husband had been talented in the arts. I would have supported him even if it meant we had to live in a tent on the beach until his talent was discovered by the world. I would never have let you waste your life, doing something you hated just for…for…*money*."

Clarissa wrinkled her nose as she said the word "money" as if it were offal and that's when John found himself going from being smitten with this beautiful woman to being head-over-heels in love with her. He would follow her anywhere and spend the rest of his time writing and living the life he had been meant to live – as an artist.

Julia let her gaze travel upward towards the others in the room and looked around once again. Something was…different, she realized. She reached down and picked up the brooch once more, gazing at it and running one finger lightly over the fine covering of dust on the center green glass stone. She left the tea set where it was. There was a small voice inside of her insisting that she get out of there…the sooner, the better. "Just find John and go!" it whispered urgently.

Head down once again, (it eased the vertigo that was now playing around the edges of her vision) she quickly began making her way towards the doorway, weaving her way through the people there. Lifting her head for a moment to mark her progress, she stopped dead in her tracks, forcing whoever had been behind her to run headlong into her back. She heard a raspy apology coming to her from a great distance away, but stood her ground as she continued staring at the gaslight sconce on the wall in front of her.

John rose in unison with Clarissa and walked around the piano bench towards her, offering his arm. She took it and smiled up at him warmly. They walked through the alcove and turned left towards the graceful spiral staircase.

As Julia left the dining room and entered the foyer she was seized by an attack of giddiness such as she had never experienced in her lifetime. She closed her eyes in an attempt to stop the room from spinning out of control around her. Then she gritted her teeth and tightened her left hand on the brooch she was still holding until the pin pierced her palm. The shock of the pain forced the spell to abate. She released her vice-like grip on the door-frame she had been gripping and opened her eyes. The moment she did, she desperately wished she hadn't.

People were still milling about speaking in quiet voices as they had been all along, but they now looked like fugitives from the grave. Skeletal faces passed by her, their musty, filthy clothing hanging in tatters and giving off an odor of death and putrefication. Julia stifled a scream as she saw a ghastly figure dressed in what was left of a top hat and tails enter through the door that she and John had come through just a short time ago. His brown, leathery skin was peeling from his face, revealing the dirty white cheekbone underneath. He was arm-in-arm with a woman dressed in the remains of a wedding dress. She held a bouquet of thorny stems. She kept attempting to adjust her dress which was continually slipping off one shoulder due to the fact that the shoulder was barren of flesh. A small group of figures (Julia couldn't justify calling them "people" any longer) gathered around the couple and though she could no longer understand their croaky articulations, she understood that congratulations were being offered.

When a strong arm slipped around her shoulder protectively, Julia almost fainted with relief.

"John," she said simply, the air rushing from her lungs. She hadn't even realized that she'd been holding her breath since the "bride and groom" had entered. She turned to her husband and her eyes widened as her mouth opened in a silent scream.

It was a man...or at least it had been at one point in time. One arm, the one he had slipped around Julia remained in-tact, and that was about all. Ragged patches of hair clung to the naked bone of a skull, and gold teeth twinkled at her from bare jawbones which opened and closed spasmodically. Julia comprehended that he was attempting speech, but all the delicate organs that control that particular body function had long ago ceased to exist. She watched, wide-eyed with terror as he placed a skeletal hand upon her arm and turned his skull so that she could see his left side and the ragged remains of an ear. Surprise jolted her as she saw that his skull had been caved in. A brown substance (dried blood?) and chunks of hair clung to (and probably held together, she realized) the jagged pieces of bone. Gasping for breath and vaguely wondering why she had not yet suffered a heart attack, Julia shook her head at the creature. What was she to do? He was long since dead. She could not do anything to reverse his particular predicament.

He dropped his hand from her arm, but guided her firmly through the room with his one arm still around her shoulder. Julia had barely enough strength to place one foot in front of the other as her escort shambled beside her, navigating her through what she felt surely had to be hell.

The stairs were old and rotted through in places, but Julia grasped the banister and hoped for the best as she was led upward. That the dust on the treads had been recently disturbed by the footsteps of another vaguely registered in a corner of her conscious mind.

As Julia reached the upstairs landing, she was met with yet another shocking scene. Her husband, her John was tenderly embracing something from the other side of the grave.

Her rage becoming stronger than her fear, Julia found her voice and her strength returning with a vengeance.

She tore herself free from her praetorian guard and launched herself across the gap that lay between them just as John's par amour raised a bony arm over her head. The force of Julia's body slamming into him took John off his feet at the same time as the cadaver swung the Malacca cane in a high arc. The weapon missed its mark and instead splintered the wood of the rail that John had been leaning on and split the balustrade in two. Julia, holding onto her husband, attempted to roll the two of them out of the way of the cane that was once again descending in its deadly arc. Anticipating the blow, she attempted to shield both their heads with her bare arms.

The blow never came.

Julia looked up and saw her former macabre chaperone grappling with what was left of the piano playing siren and began scrambling out of harm's way, dragging John with her. When she had managed to put some distance between them, she grabbed hold of the rail and pulled herself to her feet.

"John, come on," she grunted, attempting to pull him up. He was like a big, stuffed doll – eyes wide and distant.

"Oh, I'm sorry to do this, but we need to get out of here and I can't carry you…"

With this, Julia hauled back with all her strength and slapped John across the face. The sound of the blow resounded like a whip-crack on the landing. His head rocked violently back. The sudden intake of breath and confusion in his eyes told her all she needed to know.

"John…come on…now," she hissed, glancing over his shoulder in the direction of the two struggling cadavers.

John rose obediently and followed Julia's rapidly descending figure down the other side of the staircase. Apparently, the "sale" was still going strong as there were creatures in all stages of decomposition still milling about in the foyer. Julia and John managed to side-step around them and reach the door. It was then that Julia realized that she was still clutching the brooch.

"I've never taken anything in my life that didn't belong to me, but I've earned this one," she said through gritted teeth.

"Come on, John. We're not out of here yet!"

John shook his head trying to clear it as he lurched drunkenly behind Julia through the door and back towards their car. No one tried to stop them. The night air smelled incredibly sweet and they both breathed deeply as they ran, grateful to be out of the little piece of Hades they had stumbled upon.

Julia slid behind the wheel and started up the big car as John climbed in beside her. She threw the gear into "Drive" and loosened pebbles flew out from under the spinning tires as she gunned the powerful engine.

With a sidelong glance, she could sense, rather than see the frown creasing her husband's brow.

"John, it's OK. We're out."

John shook his head slowly.

"I can't remember what happened," he said slowly. "The last thing I remember is you saying that you were going to go into the other room to look...look at a jewelry box, and then that woman playing the piano started talking to me. Her name was...Clarissa Montgomery. And then...I just don't remember any more...until you tackled me."

Julia grinned to herself.

"Believe me, John. You don't need to remember what happened in there, but I suspect that you might just remember in your dreams...or nightmares. Why don't you just rest right now, hon? We'll talk tomorrow. Thank God there *is* a tomorrow for us."

PART FOUR

"Yes...yes...here it is kids."

Anke struggled to turn her book so that both John and Julia could see it. It was a sketch of the brooch…*their* brooch…the brooch that decidedly was *not* a costume piece! It had been given to Clarissa Ward by her fiancé, Roland Montgomery as a wedding gift, the accompanying text explained. It had been passed down in the family to the eldest son for five generations, and each had given it to his bride-to-be. The tradition had ended with Roland though because the brooch had mysteriously disappeared after his death. He had, apparently, met his end when he was thrown from a horse and had hit his head upon a rock. He had gone into a coma from which he never recovered. His wife, Clarissa had remarried sometime thereafter, but Roland's family was outraged that the brooch had never been returned to the family. Clarissa had never given Roland any children to pass the jewelry on to, but Roland's younger brother, Maximillian wished to pass it on to his eldest son and keep the piece in the family.

It was rumored that Clarissa and her new husband Claude decided to go on a belated honeymoon trip about a year after they married, and were aboard the ill-fated Titanic when she met her watery end. Roland's family searched every inch of their dead son's home after Clarissa's death, but never found the brooch. Eventually, as the family died out, the brooch was forgotten.

"How did it end up in the 'Lineage of Antiquities'?" John asked.

"Well, Roland's mother never believed that he fell off a horse. After his death, she put an ad in the paper with a reward of fifty thousand dollars to anyone who could come up with the brooch – no questions asked! She figured Clarissa would sell it to someone and so throw the shadow of doubt over herself but, it never happened. And then, a little over two years later, Clarissa was dead anyway.

"This book deals with a lot of oddities like that. It's the *lineage* of the piece, not necessarily the value that Welheimer was interested in.

"So, do I get to ask now?" Anke said, grinning.

"What question is that?" Julia responded innocently.

"Ah hah…so it's going to be like that, is it? OK. I'll play along. Just exactly where and how did you acquire this piece?" Anke asked, turning over the brooch in her hand.

"You know, Anke," John said. "I don't think you would ever believe it."

"Just try me, John. I've heard it all!"

"Well, Anke, my friend," Julia said, "I can unequivocally guarantee that you've never, *ever* heard this one before."

THE END

APPETITE FOR LOVE

She was five hundred and fifty pounds if she was an ounce. She liked to refer to herself as "pleasingly plump." In truth, she cared about pleasing no one and had passed "plump" several hundred pounds ago.

And, she knew it.

And…she didn't care.

At thirty-three years old, Trudy was a small-minded, acrimonious, rather wretched person; not beyond a bit of treachery now and again, and usually, more often than not.

She catered to a clientele that was considered somewhat eccentric by most standards. They were men who enjoyed sexual forays with "professional" women who were exceedingly well-endowed.

Women who, like Trudy, allowed their soft, fleshy bodies to be kneaded and…needed…for a price.

Trudy procured two hundred and fifty dollars an hour for making herself available to this special breed, so anyone who wanted to put her down (if that were humanly possible) had better check out her bank account which was presently in the high six-figure range. There were, Trudy would dare say very few if any, of her counterparts in the profession who could boast of *that* kind of security.

Oh yes, she had lots of security, but not terribly much of a lot of other things.

Personality, for instance.

Trudy was of the volition that personality was not a job requirement for her. She had the correct equipment. She let herself be prodded and suckled and ogled by these freaks. She knew all the right things to do to them to keep them coming right on back for more – and that, good friends, was quite enough. If they wanted any mushy crap, they could go home to their wives or whatever bimbo was in their own bed.

Trudy lowered her nude bulk onto a chair set before a tri-fold mirror in her "private" bedroom. There were three bedrooms in the mid-size Victorian she called home. One bedroom was almost pristine in nature, and that one was hers alone. It was the antithesis of the persona she projected. It was painted soft lavender with a wide border of muted purple and yellow hydrangeas six inches from the ceiling. The sheer, tab curtains repeated the hydrangea pattern, and puddled softly onto the thick, purple carpeting. The furniture was whitewashed oak and the king sized sleigh bed boasted a luxurious lavender silk duvet, with countless pillows tossed casually at its head. Twin armoires dominated the huge room opposite her bed. One was filled to capacity with what she liked to call her working uniforms: teddies, nightgowns, camisoles and boudoir dress in every color and style imaginable. One large drawer was reserved strictly for her leather gear.

The other armoire held an entertainment system with a fifty-inch flat screen TV, Blu-Ray player, surround-sound stereo system and a state-of-the-art computer. Flowers abounded throughout. Trudy loved flowers, and loved being surrounded by their scent. The Sovereign Florist, located downtown, had a standing order to deliver four dozen of the season's best flowers to her every other day. A special messenger would deliver the new and remove the old. As much as Trudy loved flowers, she also hated to see them die.

The next smaller bedroom was rather ordinary save for the round bed centered in the room which boasted a round mirror of equal size on the ceiling. The wallpaper in here was a soft green stripe with a blood-red rose pattern scattered through, and the duvet was rich red velvet. The pillows were stacked up in the center of the bed. The only illumination came from the countless candles that bordered the walls on delicate, spindle-leg tables and small glass shelves, and they played a gentle, golden light on everything they touched. This was for those few, rather conventional clients who went for straight sex and maybe a little slap and tickle.

The last bedroom was decorated in early dungeon with chains, whips and iron rings adorning the walls. Trudy had discovered that a bed in here was anti-climactic and had had it removed. In actuality, it was the most popular room of all. Those clients who liked to frequent that room liked to think that once they had Trudy chained to a wall, she was at their mercy. In fact, however, Trudy alone knew the trick of escaping from each and every source of bondage in the room, and it was they who were at her mercy when they chose this particular type of excitement. It never ceased to amuse her how many men who, otherwise exemplifying "normality" (whatever the definition for "normal" was currently), had deviancies beyond the scope of imagination of their families and friends.

Trudy examined her face closely. She had been considered quite pretty once, with her dark, sparkling eyes, white, white skin and thick, glossy, almost black hair. There was a time ago, almost further back than Trudy could remember, when her bathroom scale registered one hundred and seventeen pounds and a lean, sleek five foot seven inch fourteen-year-old girl faced her in the mirror each morning, white teeth shining brightly in a smile. That was before she had become her "daddy's little sweetie," and before he had started making those little visits into her room in the early hours of the morning while her four brothers slept soundly. It was before…while her mother was still alive and happy and proud of her beautiful, vivacious daughter.

Now, even her mother would be hard-pressed to find traces of that girl in the woman Trudy had become. Her eyes were hooded now by soft flesh and their sparkle had long since been replaced by a churlish gleam. Her smooth skin was still white enough, but had taken on a pasty pallor, born of too little sunshine and too many nights spent in a drug-induced haze. Her hair, although still thick, had dulled somewhat and had more shades of blonde than a Clairol commercial.

She had been automatically fondling her nipples while she sat and was pleased to notice how quickly they responded to her touch. They stiffened a lot quicker than some of her clients, she noted wryly. Her right hand slipped down between her thighs. Her labia were moist and hot and she parted them seeking the small button of pleasure hidden there. Slowly, rhythmically, she began massaging herself. Her eyes closed and her breath quickened as she sought the explosion of pleasure to come with increasing urgency.

The doorbell rang echoing up from downstairs and Trudy debated momentarily whether to keep the horny bastard waiting, or to satisfy herself.

Greed won out and Trudy arose heavily, grabbing at a sheer, black robe edged with ostrich feathers. She made her way ponderously down the curving staircase one step at a time, stopped to pull her robe on over her nude body when she reached the landing, and shuffled her way to the door in her bare feet.

Her peep-hole revealed her eight o'clock client: a darkened male profile wearing a hat pulled well down over the eyes and a trench coat – collar turned up against the freezing drizzle that had just begun. "Oh shit! A Humphrey Bogart freak. And I guess he expects me to make like Lauren Bacall," Trudy mused ruefully.

She took a deep breath and opened her door for the last time.

# # #

She was being ravished in a way she'd never been. This guy was just incredible. Not one part of her body was left untouched, not one orifice went unexplored. At one point, she found herself arching her ass in the air like a cat in heat as he alternately slid his tongue along its contours and spanked her...just hard enough to make her squirm with delight. He'd paid her up-front for seven hours of her time, and the saying, "time flies when you're having fun..." began to take on new meaning. Trudy, who truly hadn't been the recipient of any male pleasure for...well, she couldn't even remember the last good fuck she'd had...found herself writhing and rolling around like a kid on her first encounter.

# # #

She awakened very slowly, the languor of sex weighing heavily upon her. The sun sliding in through the verticals warmed her cool skin. Her eyes were still closed but her mouth curled up into a smile when she recalled the pleasure she'd enjoyed the previous night, experiencing one heart-stopping, pounding, shuddering orgasm after another. And, when they were both spent, she had actually fallen asleep next to – holy shit! She still didn't know his name! Oh, well. It wasn't important anyway. The truth was, she'd had an amazing night and almost felt guilty about her own pleasure.

The veil of sleepiness began to lift and she felt an urgency in her bladder. She began to gather herself to get out of bed and discovered an inability to move. Her eyes flew open.

The night before, she'd been unable to see him clearly. He'd requested she shut the lights in the house after he'd handed her over two grand at the front door, explaining to her in his hoarse voice, that he had a problem with his eyes and he found even a dim light most irritating. And hell, that was his privilege. He'd paid very well up front and she'd seen hundreds of guys over the years with quirks and hang-ups and requests weird enough to curl your hair.

He'd insisted on getting disrobed privately in the bathroom adjoining the bedroom. While she'd waited, Trudy availed herself of a few bright orange pills which she'd chosen from the rainbow array hidden in a small drawer built into the platform of the bed. She swallowed them dry and waited for the "hit" while he carried on with whatever he was carrying on with in the bathroom. She never used liquor before seeing a client. They could smell it on her breath and some objected to her not being fully aware or fully attentive. With the pills, however, they had no clue as to how high she went and she usually needed to be pretty high to deal with the assortment of freakazoids who passed through her bedroom.

She'd vaguely taken note of the dragging sound he made as he crossed the carpet to her bed. The fact that he probably had a bad leg passed through her consciousness like a shadow and evaporated just as quickly, as she felt his weight settling on the bed. She began to roll over, toward him, and she felt him grip her wrist with surprisingly strong and bony hands and push her back to her original position flat on her back. He held her arms back and over her head as he took her and, as his breathing became labored with his quickening pace, he began to emit an odd, high-pitched keening wail. But, he never spoke. Most guys moaned or grunted or told her things they wanted her to do or to say to them, but this guy was Silent Sam, except for that wailing thing. And that was OK with her because it left her able to concentrate on her own pleasure as that big schlong pumped in and out of her overheated oven. The one time he let go of her wrists and hiked her legs up onto his narrow shoulders, she shuddered involuntarily from the cool, rather slick feeling on her calves, but her revulsion was quickly forgotten as a titillating orgasm overtook her.

Now, his body had taken on a strange, oval shape

(or had it been that way all along…)

and his head seemed to have pulled itself deeper into his shoulders. His arms

(there appeared to be two sets of them somehow…)

and legs looked to be almost the same length and his elbows and knees were protruding at strange angles. Then, there was the hair – bristling black hair all over the arms and legs and body. And he moved about constantly, restlessly, making a strange chittering noise.

Trudy's observations were made while she strained against the constraints of the thin, white, sticky thread crisscrossing over her and holding fast her ample body. Her eyes flew to the mirror suspended above the bed. The sun reflected off the viscid greenish fluid between her thighs.

As she stared at her reflection, Trudy hitched in her breath and began to scream.

His glittering eyes danced about wildly at the sound and the creature's arms and legs waved disjointedly as he fought to maintain his balance even as his body was completing its transformation.

Trudy screamed even louder now – a continuous, shattering howl. It was impossible for her to move or even lift her head as she lay akimbo on the bed upon which she'd made her living and, upon which apparently, she would now be engaged in the business of dying.

The creature was making its way towards her slowly. Its contorted body shuffled along now on six legs, mandibles slamming open and shut madly, eyes rolling in its bullet head.

"Get away from me, you son-of-a-bitch! Get the fuck away from me!"

She glared balefully at the thing and she heard herself whimpering in abject terror as the thing drew ever closer.

"N…n…noooooo….."

The thing began to clamor aboard her now, twitching and chittering incessantly.

She felt its hard, armored shell scraping her belly and her thighs and she could smell its fetid breath as it twisted its horrible face closer to hers. The beetle-black eyes were fathomless and cold as it inspected her horror-struck face. Its mandibles closed down and ripped away part of her left cheek, and she watched, terror-crazed as her own blood sprayed onto its mottled brown thick shell.

Trudy screamed – her wailing teetered on the edge of insanity now as her mind began gleefully slip-sliding. Insanity was gaining by leaps and bounds as the thing slid down and jabbed its mandibles into her left breast while probing the heat between her legs.

Trudy had a perfect over-view of her last few minutes of life and part of her registered amazement at the fact that suddenly, she was very detached from her hopeless situation. She had heard, somewhere, that under extraordinary circumstances, the mind is capable of fleeing to another zone in order to protect itself. It seemed to her then that her circumstances were indeed extraordinary.

Any semblance of humanity the creature had once displayed was now replaced by its crazed, insectile guise. It lanced into the soft, white flesh of her massive belly as Trudy's last hold on sanity slid away. Blood sprayed freely everywhere and the wallpaper took on a new pattern.

The creature began its feeding frenzy in earnest now, noisily sucking on the gray intestines roping out from the huge gouge above her navel. It hadn't eaten in such a long time, and mating gave it such an unearthly appetite....

THE END

FULL CIRCLE

PART ONE

The rage that coursed through him fed upon itself like a brushfire – scorching everything in its path. All semblance of reason had retreated to the furthermost corners of his mind, cowering there while waiting for this latest volley of violence to pass. There was going to be a long wait.

What had triggered this latest episode was a small, rather innocuous pink slip of paper. It had been folded neatly in half and attached to today's paycheck, which had been triple its usual amount, due to the fact that two-week's severance pay had been included.

Jack Shikker was definitely not a happy man. This was the fourth time in as many years that he'd been ousted from a position. Granted, these positions were beneath him. He was writing lousy press releases for third-rate accounts at a third-rate ad firm, but since his references were rather wooly – albeit through no fault of his – this was the best he was able to do. Ultimately, he felt, his true talent would be recognized, and then he would show the world just what he was capable of doing. And that time wasn't far into his future. You could make book on that.

As for his present position, he'd been waiting for the other shoe to drop since last Tuesday. He'd gone nose to nose with the head of his department. That jerk-off didn't know shit from Shinola anyway, so who cared? Jack had been asked to meet a client at Newark International Airport earlier that day and deliver her back to the office. He had decided, instead, to pitch an idea of his own to the client and show the fools who ran the public relations department just how good he was. Might even get himself a raise – or possibly even a nice promotion, he'd thought. Maybe both!

In retrospect, he felt he should have realized that it was going to be a fucked-up day.

He had carefully checked himself out in his car's rear view mirror as he sped eastward along Route seventy-eight in New Jersey. A few extra pounds had graced his middle recently, but that was OK. It only added to his imposing, commanding figure, he reasoned. He brushed thick fingers through his wavy blonde hair, and smiled broadly, checking out his even, white teeth. Yep! You still got it kiddo, he thought, as he admired his image. He swerved slightly to avoid side-swiping a brown Toyota in the lane next to him and answered their blaring horn by shooting his left arm out the window, middle finger pointed high in salute.

"Why don'cha learn how to drive, asshole?" he said loudly to accompany the salute. "God-damned old farts shouldn't be behind the wheel, anyway," he muttered.

He'd met the client at Newark International Airport and filled in the drive time with idle talk about the weather, the New Jersey Devils and himself...mostly himself, embellishing a bit on his accomplishments – for the flow of the story. He then took her to an exclusive restaurant on Lexington Avenue frequented by high power advertising types. Delgado's was famous amongst the crowd because in a business where secrets were closely guarded, privacy was ensured due to the clever layout of booths, luxurious thick carpeting, heavy draperies and well-disguised acoustical ceilings. The atmosphere in the restaurant was that of a well-appointed den. He wanted to impress her with his choice of restaurants because this client happened to be CEO and President of Jeunesse Dorée a very large and still-growing firm which his agency had been romancing for over four months. Alexis Reinhold was a former cover girl and runway model and still an attractive woman in her early fifties. She had represented the line of Jeunesse cosmetics when she was just starting her modeling career and, twenty years later when she'd heard that they were going belly up, decided to put some of her considerable assets behind the failing company. Her determination and savvy brought the faltering line to where it was today – a multi-million-dollar corporation that had expanded to include hair and nail products and now, a line of women's intimate apparel.

Jack wined and dined her, slipping in a few watery compliments to grease the wheels. They were probably the best she'd heard in years anyway, Jack reasoned, and coming from someone who was twenty years her junior, she should be flattered. She matched him drink for drink that afternoon and listened politely to his sales talk, as she nibbled on her crab salad. She asked him if this was what his agency had in mind when they told her they had a dynamic presentation that was sure to impress her. When he told her in a voice, now thick with the effects of alcohol consumption, that this was *his* brainchild, she laughed, thanked him for his time and started to rise from her chair. He grabbed her by her wrist then, and suggested that if she didn't like that idea, he had another. She looked at him, amusement dancing in her emerald green eyes.

"And, pray tell, just *what* might that idea be, Mr. Shikker?"

He looked at her, eyes narrowing slyly, "Well, I just thought maybe you'd like some dessert to top off this fine meal."

"Thank you, but I don't eat desserts, Mr. Shikker," she replied, in a now-guarded tone.

"Oh, but this one doesn't have many calories, and it's all protein." Grinning nastily, he slid the linen napkin off his lap to reveal his hand wrapped around the bulging erection in his trousers.

Her reaction was not what he had anticipated. She deftly twisted her wrist away from his grasp, stepped back and laughed with considerable gusto.

"Good-bye Mr. Shikker. It's been…amusing." She then turned on her heel and left as waiters and other customers craned their necks in curiosity. His mouth hung open as he stared at her departing figure through a thick filter of intoxication. Wouldn't have let her anyway, he thought maliciously. Wouldn't let her if she was the last tongue on the god-damned planet!

He finished the rest of his lobster tail and washed it down with two more Martinis. By four-thirty that afternoon, when he'd managed to roll back into the office, Marty Goldman was waiting for him and ushered Jack into his office. He silently handed him a steaming cup of black coffee and as Jack began sipping the strong brew, proceeded to chew him out from every direction. Seems the bitch had called Goldman after she'd left the restaurant. The President of the agency had also been summoned and had been forced to cancel his afternoon appointments and personally pick her up from a Manhattan street corner in his own limousine and soothe her ruffled feathers. She had whined about sexual harassment and threatened to call the police in on both Jack and the agency.

Jack had listened to Goldman's tirade for what seemed like an hour, and when he'd had enough, began gathering himself up to leave. The old man started sputtering, demanding that Jack take his seat. He then threatened Jack with dismissal, spittle flying everywhere in his rage. He'd demanded that Jack call the client and apologize, begging her forgiveness, and tell her that the whole idea had been his alone and that the agency had never known what he was planning. Goldman was leaning over his desk now, his face purple, his fist pounding the top of his desk for emphasis.

That was it! Jack drew the line at kissing ass – especially old, ugly ass.

Jack surged out of his chair and reached the account manager's desk in one long stride, grabbing the older man's tie and twisting it around his knuckles until they were pressing up against Goldman's bobbing Adams-apple. Mouth open wide in an attempt to draw in air, eyes popping, Goldman began flailing ineffectually at Jack's broad shoulders. The depth of Jack's inebriated condition had struck Goldman a fraction too late.

Jack shook the manager a few times by the tie he was grasping and then stopped suddenly. His eyes drifted out of focus as he seemed to remember something. He loosened his grip, slid back from the desk, checked his watch, bid Goldman goodnight and abruptly left, staggering slightly and leaving the old man rasping and shaking.

Now today, he'd returned to the office from a nice liquid lunch and found this little surprise in his pay envelope which was propped up against a picture of Jenny and the kids on his desk. They'd been too chicken-shit to face him, so they'd just left it there.

Bastards!

Well, screw them! He didn't need their crap anyway! And besides – he'd been thinking about getting new job for a while now. Change of atmosphere would do him a world of good! Find a place where his talents were appreciated!

His fleshy mouth twisted into an ugly grin as he sped along the darkening highway.

# # #

Rachel Whelan held her daughter's hand as they walked home. It was getting a bit late, but it was summer, so at eight-twenty in the evening, the darkness had not yet settled in. Rachel smiled as she looked down at her daughter, stroking the warm top of her head. The golden ponytails on either side of her face were caught up by two sparkly clown berets – Amanda's all-time favorites. The little girl was chattering incessantly about the books she had chosen for herself at the library, and the twin ponytails wagged up and down in her excitement.

"Right, Mommy?"

Rachel pulled herself out of her reverie to reassure her daughter. At six, Amanda was a tiny, female image of her father, with tawny blonde hair, deep-set blue eyes and golden skin. Rachel pushed a stray lock of dark hair away from her own face. Maybe I'll go blonde after the baby's born, she mused. She had often played around with this idea, but had never had the nerve to follow through. Her sister, Gina, was a hair-stylist and had encouraged Rachel.

"Oh, just do it," she urged. "Your skin is definitely light enough, and with those light blue eyes, it will look perfect. Besides, then maybe Amanda will look more like *your* daughter instead of mine," she'd added teasingly.

Rachel had been surrounded by blondes while growing up. Both her sister Gina and her brother Jeff were blonde as were their parents. Rachel was the only child who had inherited her maternal grandmother's dark brown hair.

Rachel wondered if her new baby would look like her

or Frank. She unconsciously stroked her distended abdomen as she thought now about the baby's arrival into their little family – now only about three weeks away. They had tried for three years to have this second child and they were baffled as to why Rachel seemingly couldn't get pregnant. After all, Amanda was conceived on their honeymoon! Her doctors had told her to consider in-vitro or adoption, but she and Frank felt they wanted to keep trying the old fashioned way for a while longer, especially since all tests that had been performed on both of them had been negative – meaning there were no tangible reasons why they could not conceive.

Then, last Thanksgiving, Rachel and Frank had invited both the families for dinner at their new home. It was their first *real* home. They had lived in a lovely apartment in Marlboro until Frank had been transferred north, but as lovely as the apartment was, it wasn't a real home. Real to them meant having their own back yard with a swing set for their kids and their very own trees and flowers and an address that belonged just to them.

They had moved into their new home at the beginning of November, so they found themselves working almost night and day to get everything ready for the holidays. They had both agreed to have absolutely everyone present for their Thanksgiving feast because it was such a special holiday.

Rachel didn't think that they had forgotten *anything* for the festivities. Flowers and pumpkins abounded. And, there was probably enough food to serve a small army. There was a beautifully arranged antipasto, fragrant home-baked bread, a huge golden turkey, fresh cranberry sauce, cornbread stuffing with apple and sausage, three kinds of potatoes, six different vegetables, salad, pumpkin pie, coconut custard pie, walnut tartlets and a New York style cheesecake that Rachel had made at the beginning of the week.

That day after serving everyone, she finally sat down to eat. She skipped the antipasto, but helped herself to some turkey, stuffing and cranberry sauce. She started nibbling on the turkey and stuffing and her eyes widened in surprise. She ran for the bathroom and promptly lost the turkey, the stuffing, her breakfast and what felt like a week's worth of food. Suspecting a virus, she went to her family doctor the next day. He did an initial work-up and told her when she called later that afternoon, that she would be rid of her "virus" by the following July.

"July?" she'd repeated incredulously.

"Yup!" said Dr. Mandarin. "And it will probably weigh in at around seven or eight pounds!"

She didn't know whether to laugh, cry or jump up and down with joy – so she did all three.

And Frank had been no less jubilant.

So now, with less than a month before delivery, Rachael counted her blessings as she walked slowly along Mountain Avenue towards home and the husband she adored.

# # #

Jack aimed at the exit that would take him to his house in Berkley Heights. He hoped that Jenny and the kids weren't home yet. Maybe he could figure out a way to tell Jen that wouldn't set her off wailing about how much money they *didn't* have and what was she going to do about food and the mortgage and the kids' school and all the other crap he didn't care to hear about right now. Besides, he knew her old man could bail them out. He only *had* a million or two in the bank, and could well afford to float them for a while again.

It was misty out, and the thick, roiling fog was beginning to creep down the mountainside, making driving precarious. Jack, however, prided himself on his ability to be at one with his machine, and on his instantaneous reaction in any given situation.

"And, I'm even better when I've had a few. It just sharpens the old senses."

When he'd loudly issued that gem earlier in the day at the Duck Inn, a small, seedy bar in lower Manhattan, the bartender fished a five-dollar bill from his stained apron. He slapped it down on the bar and turned to the closest patron.

"Bet he can't even make it to the door in a straight line!" he quipped.

"I don't take sucker bets," the patron replied, and they both guffawed loudly over their private joke.

Jack's Lincoln slid the last thirty feet at the top of the exit ramp off Route seventy-eight, going six feet past the "stop" sign. He cursed mildly and gave a cursory glance to his right and slammed his foot onto the accelerator before the big car even came to a full stop. He took note of the car coming up on his left with its horn blaring angrily, and shot his left arm out the open window, middle finger pointed skyward. It was his stock response to a lot of annoying things in his life.

His foot pressed further down on the accelerator to underscore his displeasure as the westbound BMW swerved and managed to slide safely past his left rear quarter panel.

"Up yours, World!" he shouted thickly. "Up all of yours!"

# # #

Rachel was out of breath as she slowly walked up the beginning of the last steep incline on Mountain Avenue before reaching her home. The road offered very little level ground and was a series of twisting curves and hills, thereby providing most of the houses there a beautiful, natural setting. Each home was set well back from the road, with tall trees and bushes scattered liberally in front to insure maximum privacy and minimal road noise. Ordinarily, she loved walking up and down the lush hills. It was such a beautiful neighborhood. So quiet and…safe. A wonderful, peaceful place in which to raise her child – *children* – she hastily corrected and smiled at the thought.

Mother of two…

And, maybe even mother of three or four someday. She smiled to herself as she considered the possibilities.

Rachel paused for a moment to catch her breath. Oh well, I guess they didn't name it "Mountain Avenue" for no reason, she mused ruefully. And, I can definitely use the exercise. She began her ascent again and grinned at her daughter who was still chatting amiably and skipping every few steps while playing a hopping game with herself. It's just so wonderful when you're young, thought Rachel. Here, Amanda was bouncing and full of energy at the end of her day and she, while only twenty-nine, felt as if she were approaching ninety faster than a speeding bullet! I guess I can blame this on the baby, she thought cheerfully. I'm certainly not going to blame it on that chocolate bar I had last night or the milkshake I had the night before, or the half-bag of cookies from the night before that! That's OK. She brightened suddenly. After the baby comes, I'll be so busy with diapers, formula, two a.m. feedings, *and* Amanda, I'll probably be able to eat a whole pizza every night and never gain a pound.

The thought of a hot, cheesy pizza made her mouth water and she attempted to hurry her steps a bit. She hadn't eaten since two o'clock, which meant the baby hadn't eaten, and if that baby was as hungry as she was right now...

"Come on, Amanda. Let's cross over to the other side of the street. We only have another block to go. And Daddy must be wondering where we are by now."

# # #

He'd teach them! He'd teach everybody! They thought they were so damned clever, but he'd show *them* who was smarter. The fog of Jack's intoxication was thickening as rapidly as the fog on the road.

He knew for sure that Goldman was fooling around with his twenty-something secretary and come Monday, Jack was going to let everyone else in the building know the slimy little secret that the holier-than-thou pint-sized hot-shot was keeping. Treat *him* like dirt, would they? Like hell! Those bastards would pay!

A guttural, atavistic snarl issued from Jack's throat. It was a sound he was barely aware of as he fought to control the wheel of the Lincoln as it slid around the corner onto Mountain Avenue.

# # #

Sidewalks are at a premium in certain ultra-residential areas in the New Jersey suburbs, and Berkley Heights is one of those areas. The residents here walk along the edges of lawns and know enough to wear reflective colors when they walk in the evenings. Rachel and Amanda knew the drill.

They both wore white, knee-length shorts, matching hot pink sleeveless tops (which Rachel's mom had surprised them with last week) and sneakers with reflective patches in back and on the sides. Rachel also had reflective patches on the yellow canvas back-pack she carried. She believed in safety.

# # #

On a late summer night, at dusk, with a fine mist falling, and a heavy fog swirling over the roads, Jack took the familiar turns at forty-four miles an hour, contemptuous of the wuss' who had to crawl along just because driving conditions weren't ideal.

His blood alcohol level at the time was .15 and climbing by the minute due to the pint bottle he kept pulling deeply from as he drove. His anger at the world in general deepened as he drove muttering to himself all the while, recalling all those he perceived had "wronged" him in some way. The list was endless.

# # #

Rachel heard tires squealing at the top of the hill and

instinctively began ushering Amanda further onto the lawn they were walking past. The child tripped over a root protruding from the ground and lost her balance. She clutched her books tighter to her small body. She knew you had to keep library books clean, or you would not be allowed to borrow any more. She cried out in pain when her knee struck a rock as she fell. Rachel bent down awkwardly, attempting to help her daughter regain her feet.

# # #

The tires of the big Lincoln were old. They should have been cause for failure when the car was inspected three months ago, but Jack had a friend who owned a private inspection station in Patterson and said friend would hand a new inspection sticker to anyone he knew who was willing to hand him a fifty-dollar bill.

Had the tires had enough tread, and had Jack taken the turn near Cypher Lane at the recommended twenty instead of at thirty-eight miles per hour, the car may not have begun its precipitous lunge across the road.

The agonizing scream of tires being pushed to their limits brought Rachel's head up with a jolt. Her eyes widened as she saw the yawning maw of the grill-less Lincoln careening across the road, its headlights flat, dead and dark. Her own mouth opened in an answering scream.

The sound was obscene – thick and wet and rendering.

He heard, with a strange clarity, the sound of steel breaching soft tissue and splintering bone. It went on forever. And, when he thought it was over, it began again, only softer this time, as if the flesh and bone were giving in and yielding without a struggle.

The Lincoln continued its murderous advance for another twenty yards, sluicing now through a well-manicured lawn, until Jack succeeded in regaining control and maneuvered it back onto the pavement.

Heart thudding and instantly sobered, he managed to stop the car and pushed his door open. Without bothering to close it, he half-jogged, half-fell down the road (hoping against hope that he hadn't seen what he thought he saw, but somehow knowing that his worst fears would be realized.)

A sob caught in his throat as the full impact of the carnage he had wreaked struck when he caught sight of a blood-washed book lying on the road – one torn page dismally waving in the slight breeze.

What was left of a small torso was sprawled in a widening pool of blood, half-on and half-off the road. Its limbs were at impossible angles from each other, its face unrecognizable. A gaping split in the torso revealed secreted parts of the human body that no one had any right to view. Grey entrails were roping out and slowly slithering onto the dark, wet pavement. Disoriented, Jack gazed about and saw another body strewn thirty feet away, on the other side of the road. Jack approached, drawn almost hypnotically by the savagery of the scene, but he nevertheless recoiled as he heard a small mewling sound coming from the decimated corpse. The body suddenly seemed to be coming back to life, because there was movement under the bloodied shirt which was almost totally ripped away from the mangled chest.

The sound came again – only louder this time – more insistent. A macabre curiosity overtook him, and against his own will, he inched his way closer to the source.

He was about three feet from the bloodied remains now, and the tiny cry was distinct. His mouth was hanging open stupidly and he blinked, attempting to clear his vision and his mind enough to explicate what he was seeing.

A tiny body lay alongside the inner leg of its dead mother, only the top of its small bloodied head and one wrinkled arm visible. It was fighting for life against all odds by attempting to make its arrival into a cold, hard world known. Its cry was small and strident, but it did not know that its only possible hope for survival was too cowed to bestow assistance.

Jack turned away, eyes widening in dawning horror. His mind was fighting to keep its balance and his breathing was coming in short, jagged gasps. Even in his fear, however, he realized his predicament t and looked around furtively to make sure no one had run out of their house to see what had happened. He saw no one, but allowed that it did not mean that he was in the clear. Someone could be watching him from the darkened windows of one of the surrounding houses. He ducked his head low and staggered headlong back to his car. His unsteadiness now, however, was shock-related, rather than alcohol-induced. A deep-seeded fear was beginning to cloud his vision and push its way to the forefront of his mind. It was an instinctual fear for his own skin. He slammed his car door shut, unconsciously banging down the lock while throwing the shift lever into Drive.

Jack took a deep, shuddering breath and pulled away carefully. Careful was what he had to be now that his own life could be at risk. Taking the next two left turns, he pulled safely into his own driveway.

Getting out of the car again, he stumbled around to the front of the Lincoln, able to see by the glow of the weak light emanating from his open garage door. His stomach roiled at the sight of the fresh blood spattered and smeared over the hood, and torn, bloodied scraps of cloth caught on the rusted chrome of the bumper. He pulled out the garden hose kept by the side of the garage and turned it on.

A half-hour later, he pulled the Lincoln into the garage, next to his wife's car. After powering the garage doors closed, he examined the car more thoroughly, under the glare of a hand-held utility lamp. He satisfied himself that, for the most part, no blood could be discerned and if any remained, it would not even be noticed by anyone passing by. And, if someone did notice, he would just say that he had, unfortunately, hit a deer on his way home and didn't want to upset his wife or his kids with the sight of blood on his car. Cars were always hitting deer in this neighborhood, so no one would be suspicious. To be on the safe side, however, he unscrewed the overhead light and pocketed the bulb, throwing his side of the garage into deep shadow.

He decided that on Sunday morning, when things had quieted down, he would, after switching license plates with his wife's car, drive the car to his buddy's place in Patterson and have him add it to his growing collection of rust heaps out back. Jack would tell him that he'd gotten a big promotion and had decided to treat himself to a newer model. He'd give Jenny the same story and tell her to ask her old man to lend him some dough as an advance on his upcoming new salary. After all, a guy in his position needed to be driving a later model car anyway – maybe a nice new SUV. All that wining and dining of clients he was going to do had to be done in style.

That decision made, he closed the door between the garage and the kitchen, lumbered thru the mud room into the bathroom beyond and vomited until he was purged.

# # #

Six months had passed since that night and Jack had long since forgotten the details of the carnage he had wreaked. He had convinced himself that it was, after all, the woman and her kids' fault. If they had stayed at home at that time of night the way they were supposed to, then they would not have gotten in the way of his car.

He had checked the local newspapers for a while. The day after the event, the local paper had run a front page story on the tragedy, with graphic photographs accompanying it. Jack had skipped the photos – he had seen it all before, thank you very much – and had gone on to the detailed account, attempting to find out if the police had any clues or witnesses, but they apparently had neither. There was talk of tracking down the alleged homicide vehicle through the tire tracks that were left behind on the lawn of Mr. Ned Schaffer, but there really wasn't too much hope. The lawn had been thoroughly watered just hours before, making the tracks too indistinct to cast and capture. As the days went on, the incident began to take a back page to other, more recent news. If they hadn't found anything by this time, Jack reasoned, they weren't going to now. And, he was right. The next biggest story had come on the day of the funeral, when the story once again took over the front page and pictured Frank Whelan, the grief-stricken husband and father of the victims.

"I'll never rest until I find out who killed them," he had sobbed to the reporter of the Summit Register. "It had to be someone who was drunk or crazy or both, and I...I... can't believe that he took my wife and my babies from me. I'm gonna find that son-of-a-bitch...and when I do...."

Yeah, right, Jack thought. Just *you*, when the cops couldn't find anything out. Of course, the cops were all idiots, Jack reasoned, but he couldn't see this guy as being much more. He'd get over it and calm down eventually.

Jack got over it about ten days later, when there was no longer any mention of it in the newspaper.

And by now, the whole incident had faded so much in his own mind, that Jack almost felt as if it was something he had seen on a TV news report, and not something that had happened to him personally. He felt that a strong mind should be able to consider only the relevant and this issue was no longer an incident that was germane in his life.

He had moved on to yet another job, and this time had managed to find a position with Williams and Sotheby, a small advertising firm in Warren. He had stretched the truth on his job application, saying that he hadn't worked in the States for the last two years, because he had been abroad – in Spain, actually – and had worked on a small, but lucrative project for a private firm. He vaguely hinted at government involvement and an inability to give too many details. Being very short-handed at the time, and finding no one else willing to work for such relatively low pay in the field of advertising, Jack was hired. He went home that night and celebrated his victory with cheap champagne and then an even cheaper wine, followed by his usual – cheap whiskey.

PART TWO

Jenny Shikker was an invisible woman. She was one of those people in the medium range of everything…someone easily forgotten. She was rail-thin and had mousy brown hair that hung limply to her shoulders and a face deeply creased with worry lines. Even her once beautiful, almond-shaped light-brown eyes were dull and lifeless. She had the walk of someone carrying a tremendous burden – pendulous and stoop-shouldered. Jenny looked like a fifty-year-old woman who had lived a very hard life.

Jenny, was thirty-two.

She had once been considered pretty and vivacious and had even dated the captain of the football team in her senior year of high school, but the captain had gone off to UCLA in search of glory and she had been left behind. Her doting and misguided parents had strongly discouraged further education because they wanted to keep her close and because they felt she was a child of "delicate sensibilities."

They told her that the best thing she could do for herself was find a husband and give them grandchildren. Jenny did not go against their wishes because the thought of leaving home and being amongst strangers frankly terrified her and she had few ambitions. By the age of seventeen, she had graduated high school and worked as a secretary in an office in downtown Manhattan.

Six months later, when the pace became too frantic for her, she took a job at a small plumbing supply house in Trenton where she met Jack Shikker. At the time, Jack had seemed worldly to her. He told her had gone to New York University and was headed to the top in the advertising field. He had an uncle who was a top exec he told her, and he was just waiting for the right opening. The fact that he was working in the same office as she as an office manager, and was nowhere near the field of advertising, never struck her. Instead, she was awed by his good looks and by the aura of physical power that surrounded him and amazed that he took notice of her. They began by having lunch together a few times a week, but quickly progressed to seeing each other almost every evening after work and on weekends. She knew that her parents didn't approve of him, but she found the courage to stand up to them and argue in his defense, telling them that he would be famous one day and that this was someone who would love and protect her forever. They grudgingly yielded to her wishes and gave her the big, beautiful wedding they knew she'd always wanted. Jenny was the apple of their eye, and they loved her and wanted her to be happy.

Jenny and Jack married nine months after they first met and nine months after that, Jenny gave birth to their first child, Jack, Jr.

Jack, Jr. was a demanding baby and Jenny found herself frazzled and exhausted by him. Sex with Jack Sr. became almost non-existent. It had basically come to a grinding halt as soon as Jack found out she was pregnant. Her doctor had told her there was no reason not to continue having relations with her husband, but Jack had demurred saying that he didn't want to hurt the baby and as she got bigger in size, he said it would be too uncomfortable for them both. Then, after she had given birth, she was too tired all the time. She vaguely suspected that Jack was seeking satisfaction elsewhere. When she approached him timidly one night and clumsily related her suspicions, he backhanded her.

That was the first time. It was far from the last.

After that, sex became something of a chore for Jenny due to the fact that Jack attempted it most often when he was drunk. Because he was inebriated, it took forever for him to be satisfied and if he wasn't, he took it out on her and her inability to be woman enough to please him. She never approached him anymore. She had never enjoyed sex that much anyway, and now it had become such a vile, painful thing that she found the act insufferable. Now she knew what her mother had meant when she had darkly told her daughter years ago about doing her "wifely duties."

Jack, Jr. was seventeen now and he had a little sister, Emily, who was eight years his junior. He was always in some sort of minor trouble in high school, but he was an exuberant, strong-willed boy, Jenny knew, and he never got into any really serious dilemmas.

His teachers spoke to her about Jack's penchant for violence with other students, but he limited himself to fighting only with students on the opposing football teams. Only one teacher who spoke with Jenny felt that Jack's actions, even on the field were inappropriate, so Jenny chalked it up to the teacher's personality. She told herself that the teacher just didn't *like* her son.

Jack was very popular amongst his peers. He belonged to a lot of clubs both in and out of school and was always asking her for money for dues and special events that they were sponsoring. She really didn't know too much about these clubs, but did remember some from her own high school days, and didn't want him to be left out of anything. She always admonished him never to tell his father about all the money she handed him on the side. His father wouldn't like it. This was money coming to her from her father and Jack would want it for his own use and not his son's clubs. Jack, Jr. readily complied with her wishes.

Emily was her mother's pride and joy. While Jack, Jr. favored his father in looks, although definitely not in temperament Jenny thought, Emily was totally her child. She was just as Jenny had been at her age. However, her marks in school were all A's and she had a group of young friends who were as sweet and cute as she. She was always going to their houses for sleepovers, but avoided having them at her own house. Jenny knew that Emily feared her father and his drunken bouts and didn't want her friends to know of her home situation.

It was only once that Jack had struck Emily and that had been when she was four.

She had come in from playing in their backyard and had been in one of those moods that four-year-olds get into every other hour. She was tired and hot and cranky and flatly told her father "no" when he had ordered her to turn off the TV and get ready for dinner. She hadn't realized that he had been drinking, for even at that young age she knew better than to defy him when he was "not feeling well." Jack had bolted out of his armchair and slammed her into the living room wall before she could even blink. Jenny had come flying in from the kitchen when she heard her daughter scream and, after she had made sure that Emily was not seriously injured, had turned on Jack with a vengeance. She screamed at him as she had never done in her own defense and had threatened him with death if he ever touched her daughter in anger again.

"You have to sleep sometime Jack, just remember that," she had quietly told him in a voice trembling with rage. "And when you do, I swear to God Almighty, I'll get that knife out of the kitchen and I'll cut out your heart. And if you think I won't do it – guess again."

He was so taken aback by her fury, he didn't say a word. She picked up her whimpering daughter then and called her son down from upstairs and took them both with her into the car and drove off. She never returned until late the next day and when she did, she acted as if nothing had transpired. She had probably gone to her parents' house, Jack thought. Had probably thought she would scare him into thinking she would leave him, but he knew better. She wouldn't go. She would never go.

And, she wouldn't. She knew that. Just why, she didn't know. Well, maybe she did. If she left, she'd have nowhere to go except to her parents' house, and that was the last place she wanted to be with her two children. It's not that they wouldn't accept her with open arms, and they were really good people, but she didn't think she could stand the look of disappointment on her father's face, and the knowing "I told you so" look her mother would give her.

She decided that as long as she had to, she would make her life as bearable as possible by keeping away from Jack as soon as she saw the danger signals, and she would get a few extra dollars here and there from her father to help pay the bills and keep things on an even keel as much as she could, for as long as she could.

This wasn't going to be easy right now she thought with a heavy heart. She was pregnant again and Jack had told her he didn't want any more children after Emily was born. The fact that he had practically raped her and neglected to use any kind of protection in his last drunken episode totally escaped her, and would certainly never enter *his* mind. She was pregnant, abortion was not an option, and Jack would blame her. Now, she had to figure out how to tell him that in six months, there would be another child.

Jack took the news a lot worse than she imagined he would have. He had, apparently, had an argument with one of the partners of the firm and had come to within a hairs breadth of losing his job. He had left work to find that his car had been towed because of all the parking tickets he had received and neglected to pay. Finding out that Jenny was pregnant was the icing on his miserable cake. He actually wanted to physically slam her through a wall, but knew better than to do that if she was carrying a baby. It would have been a great way for her to lose it, he thought, but she had already told her parents of the upcoming event, and she was too far along anyway. If he ever wanted see another penny from those tightwads, then he had to make sure that nothing happened. But, that didn't prevent him from terrorizing her and bellowing at the top of his lungs about her fucking stupidity and her fucking negligence and how she was lucky to have someone who could put up with her fucking bullshit! It went on for over an hour while Jenny cowered in a corner and her daughter did likewise upstairs in her bedroom. It actually went on until the local police showed up at their door, following up on a complaint from one of the neighbors. One of them tried to work his way into the house, but Jack called Jenny over to show him that she was still alive and well, and he managed to keep the cops out.

After they left, Jack told Jenny he was going out for a while and stomped out the door after grabbing her car keys and his coat. Jenny heaved a sigh of relief when the door slammed shut behind him. She'd sleep in Emily's room tonight she thought, and maybe he wouldn't start up again when he came home as he sometimes did. She fervently hoped that Jack, Jr. would be home in just a short while so that he wouldn't run into his father on his way in. That wouldn't do at all.

# # #

It was past two in the morning before Jack Sr. staggered through the door. He had finally managed to convince himself, somewhere between bourbon on the rocks number six and number eleven that perhaps Jenny's being pregnant wasn't such a bad thing after all. Yeah, he'd have to put up with a lot of wailing and shit-smelling for a while again, but maybe they could convince her parents that now that they were such a large family, they needed a bigger house to live in. Maybe even a bigger car…one of those Cadillac Escalades would look nice parked in the long driveway of one of those new houses they were building in Warren. Yeah…that would be real nice.

He took another pull from the bottle of Jack Daniels that he was gripping by the neck and threw himself on the sofa in the family room, too wrecked to even attempt getting up the stairs. In five minutes, he was snoring loudly, the pint bottle of JD pouring its contents onto the carpeting from his limp hand.

# # #

Rodman, Buehler and Shikker were the best defense team that Lincoln High School had to offer. Talk was that the "Three Amigos" as they had been dubbed, had already been approached by scouts from U.C.L.A. and Notre Dame. Dallas too had made an offer, but to only two of the three and the three had made a pact to stay together. All three were troublemakers of a sort, but their antics were looked upon benignly by most of the staff. They were, after all, stars and seventeen-year-old boys and all had essentially good grades.

The boys had cause for a special celebration today. Victor Rodman turned eighteen and his two older brothers and their friends were giving Victor a blow-out birthday bash.

The party was being given at the Green Beer Bot'le, a small club in New Brunswick that catered to the college crowd from Rutgers. The Rodman brothers had hired the entire club for the night, secured special entertainment for the crowd and the services of the best DJ's in town. They'd sent out a general invitation to their whole fraternity and told Victor to invite anyone he wanted. The Amigos were more selective than their hosts, however, so they invited only members of the football team and the cheerleaders. Everyone who had been invited, from both Rutgers and Lincoln came. They knew the reputation of the Rodman's, and their parties were no less than world-class. Food, drink and sex flowed freely.

A spectacular cake – a three-dimensional likeness of the Rutgers football stadium – was rolled onto the raised dais at midnight, by six beautiful girls dressed in tuxedos. The girls removed their top hats and held them to their breasts while dramatically singing "Happy Birthday" to Victor. After their slightly off-key rendition, they slipped exquisite crystal candy dishes, filled with festively colored capsules and pills out from underneath the napkins surrounding the cake. They walked around through the crowd offering them like candy mints, while the DJ's speakers blasted out "I'm So Excited" – an old Pointers Sisters tune. By the end of the song, two-thirds of the crowd had gotten to their feet dancing wildly, thoroughly excited themselves by the combination of booze and pills that was now coursing through their young veins.

The six tuxedo-clad beauties made their way through the milling crowd on the floor, returning to the small dais where the cake had been set up. The cake had been removed and they placed their now empty crystal dishes on the bare table.

The lights went down and colored spotlights began to whirl about. Each girl in turn whooped loudly, and in pairs of two turned to face each other. Each tugged hard on the front of her partner's tuxedo which pulled smartly away revealing a totally nude body underneath, save for a bow tie adoring each neck and four-inch-high, black patent leather, platform spiked heels which clad each foot. The girls turned to face their wildly cheering audience.

Other bodies, in various stages of nudity, both male and female, poured in from doors surrounding the room. Lights were dimmed even lower while the red, blue, yellow and green spotlights continued to spin dizzyingly about. The orgy, for it could now truly be called an orgy, continued until four in the morning. Dazed, drunk and disoriented kids between the ages of sixteen and twenty-two staggered out into the parking lot that night. Most of the sixty or so kids who'd stayed till the end of the debauchery, opted to sleep it off in their cars when the club closed its doors. Three cars left the lot simultaneously. One was driven by Jim Portman, one of George Rodman's best friends. Another was driven by Pamela Jamison, head cheerleader and sometimes girlfriend of Jack Jr. The three Amigos occupied the third vehicle.

Jim Portman had refused the pills but not the booze that had been passed around. He managed to drive all the way to his home without incident. Once there, however, he passed out cold in his mother's pansy bed and was discovered there by her the next morning when she went out to pick up her morning paper. By six that evening, twenty-year-old Jim had lost his driving privileges for six months, and military school was seriously being discussed between his parents, who were ignoring his very loud protestations.

Pamela Jamison and the two other girls she was driving home had not been so lucky. Close to her friend Diane's home, Pamela lost control of her Mustang when she instinctively veered her car to the left in an attempt to avoid a deer who had stepped out into the road. The Mustang skidded and slid broadside into an oak tree. The oak proved to be mightier than the Mustang, leaving Pamela minus her left leg,

Diane with a concussion that removed most of her long-term memory and Morgan, the third passenger, with a broken jaw and a mouthful of splintered and missing teeth, along with various contusions and several broken bones.

Victor Rodman, Todd Buehler and Jack Shikker stumbled back into Todd's Chevy Trail Blazer after Todd finished yakking up his six o'clock dinner and everything thereafter. They'd had to pull over less than a mile after leaving the Club.

"Fuckin' A man…are you finally through?" I thought you were gonna puke up a lung."

"Fuck you Shikker," Todd retorted shaking his head to clear it while using his sleeve to wipe at his chin. "It was somethin' I ate before I got here. My fuckin' mother made spaghetti and meatballs and she's the shittiest cook on the planet."

"Oh yeah, man," Victor agreed readily. He belched loudly and the car filled with the smell of stale beer and onions.

"Oh shit, man…keep it to yourself," Todd groaned as he pulled a face. "Or I'll puke in your shoes." He guffawed loudly at his own wit. "But you're right," he continued. "She is the *worst* goddamned cook I ever met. She could fuck up a peanut butter and jelly sandwich!"

"Hey, Shikker," Victor called from the back seat. "Did

you get any tonight?"

"None of your fuckin' business," Jack replied mildly.

"Ahhh, up yours too," Victor said, laying down on the back seat of the Chevy. "I don't feel too good myself. I'm just gonna chill out here for a while and see…and…" His voice trailed, leaving his thought unfinished.

"Goddamn Rodman never could hold a freakin' beer." Jack commented.

"Fuck him too," Todd said.

Todd pulled the car out onto the road once more and skidded on gravel as he gunned the motor to pick up speed. He quickly regained control and pulled into the right lane as he headed onto Route twenty-two traveling at seventy-five miles per hour.

It began to rain around four-forty-five in the morning – lightly at first and then hammering the roof and hood of the truck with enough force to awaken Victor who had been snoring loudly in the back seat. He sat up for a moment, blinking stupidly at his surroundings and then flopped back down, asleep almost instantly.

Todd snickered as he saw Victor's head pop up and then down again.

"Goddamned asshole," he commented, voice thick.

"Yeah, sure…whatever," Jack said, yawning hugely. "Whatever…"

They had been driving for about twenty minutes and home was still another thirty miles away, via the back roads. They'd pulled off Route twenty-two after only one exit due to the fact that Todd had spotted two police cars parked on the shoulder of the road, giving out tickets to errant drivers. Todd wasn't taking any chances. Jack and Todd had fallen silent in the front seats. Jack was slowly drifting into sleep and Todd was fighting to keep his eyes open as the rain continued to pour.

# # #

This, like every other night since he lost his family had been a sleepless night for Frank Whelan. He had awakened from his dream drenched in the same cold sour sweat – a cry of anguish catching in his throat. In that dream, he was walking in a field of flowers. He could smell their sweet scent and feel the warmth of the sun on his skin. He could see Rachel and Amanda and a baby – a little girl, perhaps six months old. The three were on a blanket sitting amongst a spread of wild daisies. Rachel was waving at him and Amanda was standing on the blanket, jumping up and down in her excitement. He could hear the baby chortle.

Suddenly, as he watched them, he was overcome by a feeling of disquiet. He couldn't understand why. Nothing had changed. The air was still sweet. The sun was still warm on his back. But, it was wrong. Wrong for them to be there. He began to run.

He ran flat out. He could feel his heart pumping mightily with his effort and the muscles in his legs strained with his long stride.

He came no closer to them despite his effort.

Thinking crazily that he had gotten caught, somehow, on a treadmill he looked down, but the green grass was passing smoothly under his pumping legs.

He looked up to find that Rachel, Amanda and the baby were even further away than they were before.

He began shouting to them – to get away, to run, to hide, to get off that goddamned blanket, stop waving and run…anywhere…please…because something was going to happen. Something horribly bad. Something that he was powerless to stop.

He was still running to them when it happened.

Before his eyes, his family turned to stone.

The stone turned to ashes.

The ashes blew away in a sudden breeze.

Frank stopped running and he screamed for his family to come back, but the ashes that were now blowing thickly around him caught in his throat and all he could manage was a choking cry of pain.

That was his dream…his nightmare…his life now without the ones he loved.

He had wanted to end his life so many times, but he couldn't. He felt he was a coward because, despite his abject misery, he was afraid to die. And he was in a quandary because he was even more afraid to live.

Frank turned towards his bedside clock. It was three-fifty-five in the morning. Sleep was beyond him now. It always was after the dream/nightmare. Resignedly, Frank swung his feet out of the bed and stood. He padded into the bathroom, splashing cold water onto his face and neck, then looked up into the mirror. He did not recognize the face in the mirror – haggard and drawn, with dark circles under the troubled eyes. Frank shook his head to rid himself of the vision and dressed quickly and grabbed his wallet and his car keys from the table beside the front door. Shoving the wallet into his back pocket, he clambered down the stoop and got into his Volvo S60, barely glancing at the Chevy Suburban which was parked in front of him in the driveway. That had been Rachel's car. The one that was never used now.

He threw the car into reverse and had begun backing up when he noticed the rain for the first time. He waited until he was in the street to put the wipers on. The rain was only a minor inconvenience. He needed to go for a drive. He couldn't sleep and he couldn't stay in the house anymore, just lying there and thinking about his life now – or lack thereof. A drive would help focus his concentration and maybe he could stop thinking about Rachel and Amanda and their unborn child. Yeah…right…and maybe he could find the guts to exit this goddamned life and finally and forever stop feeling before he went completely and totally insane.

# # #

The sound of the blaring horn startled Todd into driving off the shoulder of the road and onto the wet and slippery grass. He shouted a string of expletives as he attempted to control his vehicle and steer it back onto the highway before the trees coming up on his right exploded into his windshield.

The sound of his startled shout and the sudden lurching of the car brought his front seat passenger to attention while his rear seat passenger continued to snore placidly.

"What the hell are you doing, Todd?" Jack shouted. "You fuckin' trying to kill us?"

"Fuck off!" Todd replied, breathing hard now that the danger was over. He could literally feel the adrenalin pumping through his veins. Sweat had popped out on his forehead despite the relative cool of the cabin.

"Guy cut me off back there. Asshole should learn how to drive."

"Yeah, man. Half of 'em shouldn't have a license." Jack agreed after only a slight hesitation. He settled down into his seat again, eyes already closing.

"Yeah, half of 'em…" Todd muttered, still shaken.

# # #

Frank drove south on Mountain Avenue, the small car taking the unremitting curves with ease. He was depending on the drive to clear his head. Focusing on his driving might do that. It always did the trick when he was younger. He went for a lot of drives once he had his license. A few before he had secured that particular bit of paper too.

His home life when he was a kid had not been the greatest. His father was a passive alcoholic who was never physically abusive to his wife and only son. The mental pressure, however, was profound. He would just drink and quietly pass out in his easy chair. Because of this, there was a pervasive air of stress that affected both Frank and his mom. There was stress because of money and more tension was created because his mother constantly strove to reform her husband, and was consistently unsuccessful in her efforts. Further pressure ensued because she expected, and not unreasonably, to have a husband and a father for her child and had neither.

Frank's mother, Nora had worked hard all her life, taking care of her ailing mother before she married, and then supporting her own family when her husband could no longer work. Frank, Sr. had been a house painter by profession. He fell off a ladder while on a job one day when Frank was only seven. He had not been drinking at this particular time or Nora probably would have packed up her son and left him. As it was, Nora was left to support the family as best she could. Having been left with no choices, she left her son at home in his father's care and got a job at the local hospital as a dishwasher.

Taking note of her red hands and raw knuckles, Frank asked her when he was about eight why she washed dishes for a living.

She'd turned to him and smiled gently. "Why, because they're dirty, of course, and someone has to do it now, don't they?"

Frank had studied her closely for a moment and then, satisfied with her answer, turned and went back to playing with his set of trains.

Nora died four months to the day before he married Rachel.

His father stopped drinking the day his wife passed away. When Frank took notice of this and mentioned it to his father a few weeks later, his father simply said, "Nora wouldn't approve."

He followed his wife to the grave two months afterward.

Frank was alone. As he drove, that fact bore itself into his mind like a steel drill. Flashbacks of his family life ran through his head like a slideshow played on high speed. He wondered whether this drive had been a good idea. All his ghosts seemed to be going along with him this time.

# # #

Jack Shikker, Jr. awoke with a start. It took him a minute to realize that he was in Todd's car. He'd been having a dream. Something about a fire and a field of flowers. He turned towards Todd, rubbing the sleep out of his eyes as he did.

"Hey, man. How much further we gotta go?"

Todd did not answer.

"Hey. You deaf or somethin'? How much further…"

Jack stopped in mid-sentence, realizing with a horror that swept over him like a tidal wave that Todd, with eyes wide open, was sleeping.

The speed limit on Freemont Road in Mountainside is forty miles per hour. Frank never exceeded the speed limit, but he decelerated slightly on the turns. He was a good driver who'd never had a ticket or an accident. He felt total confidence in his ability while behind the wheel of his small machine.

Jack screamed Todd's name as he saw the guardrail rushing towards them. When Todd fell asleep, his leg had relaxed, pressing the accelerator almost all the way to the floor. The Trail Blazer was doing eight-three miles per hour going uphill.

Todd jerked awake at the sound of his name, but awoke disoriented and pulled the wheel hard to the left.

The rain that had fallen left the two-lane mountain road slippery and so, when Jack grabbed the wheel in order to avoid heading into oncoming traffic and the wall of the mountain that the road was carved from, he overcompensated and the car began to careen from one lane to the other, barely missing the guardrail on one side and the mountain on the other.

Frank rolled down his window as he drove. He welcomed the cool, damp night air that fanned his hair and face and took deep breaths of the stuff. He felt calmer now. The long drive was finally beginning to do its work.

Because Todd had been so suddenly roused out of his inebriated sleep, he was not only confused, he was also pissed-off. When he felt Jack fighting him for control of the wheel, his first instinct was to pull it back. He knocked into his friend with his right elbow to force Jack to release his grip. The struggle between the two caused the vehicle to swerve left into the oncoming lane.

Frank strained to see through the rain as his wipers cleared the glass. There was a car coming in the opposite direction, a truck actually, if he could judge by the height of its headlights, and it was swerving wildly from one side of the road to the other. Frank's heart began to hammer. There was nowhere to go.

Todd had managed to slow the speed of the SUV, and was fighting to regain control. Jack had finally relinquished his hold, but too late. The Trail Blazer was literally bouncing off the side of the mountain wall and into the path of an oncoming car.

Frank's first instinct had been to swerve out of the way of the oncoming truck, but at the last moment, a calm overtook him. He took a deep breath and held onto the wheel. Maybe this was where his ghosts had been trying to lead him.

"Steady as she goes," he muttered to himself. "Only a few more seconds…"

If Todd's judgment had not been impaired, he would not have turned the wheel so hard to the right in order to avoid the oncoming car. But he did and so the truck swerved, and rose up shakily on its two right wheels. It shot across the road and leaned even further onto its side. The screams of the passengers inside could be heard reverberating off the walls of the ravine as the Trail Blazer gained deadly momentum on the downhill and ripped through the steel guard rail. Airborne now, and seemingly in slow motion, the truck plummeted nose first in a graceful arc over the trees below. Landing on an old construction road, the big truck bounced then rolled over and over before landing on its roof where it rocked wildly like an amusement park ride. Seconds later, gas trickling from the ruptured tank ignited from a spark, bloomed and exploded, engulfing the truck in flames.

It had been forty-five seconds since Jack Shikker, Jr. had awakened from his dream of flowers and flames.

Frank's mouth dropped involuntarily as he watched the car sail sideways over the edge of the road and its headlights disappear. It was then that he realized that not attempting to avoid the car was probably what had saved his life. Had he swerved his own car, the oncoming vehicle would have, most probably, crashed into him and taken him too over the side of the mountain road.

# # #

Jack Shikker, Sr. was not a good father but when he received the news about his son's death from the somber looking sheriff who knocked at his door at six-twelve that morning, he displayed an overwhelming grief. Some of that grief was truly for his son, but some of that grief was mixed with anger at his wife, for not having more control of their son and at himself for not having more forcefully controlled them both.

It was four days before the bodies of the boys were released from the coroner's office. On the evening of the sixth day, a closed casket memorial service was held at Morningside Funeral Home in Berkley Heights. Jenny's parents had made the arrangements. Jack did not have the money to bury his own child.

When Jenny had been told of her son's death, she barely reacted. She did react, however, to her husband's increasing agitation. She took her daughter and stayed with her parents. Jack had been drinking steadily since receiving the news and Jenny wanted neither herself nor her daughter anywhere in the vicinity of his fury. Plus, she'd discovered that her son's college fund, to which her parents had contributed considerably, was totally depleted. She'd found this out after having gone to the funeral home to make her sons final arrangements. Thinking that she could use his college fund for the funeral, she'd gone to the bank and spoken to the bank manager, who was a friend of her father.

"I'm sorry, Jenny," Mr. Ryder had said in a sympathetic voice. "I don't want to add to your pain, but that account was closed almost a year ago. Your husband came in and said he was taking it out to invest and that Jack, Jr. wouldn't need a college fund anymore because there would be plenty of money."

Jenny had politely thanked Mr. Ryder and left the bank. She gripped her daughter's hand as she left and climbed back into the taxi that had taken her to the bank. She didn't bother going back to her house. She went straight to her parents' home. Once there, she gave in to the grief that she'd been holding at bay. Safe and secure and alone in her old room, sobs shook her slender body for hours as she mourned the death of her firstborn child. She knew in her heart then that her life with her husband was over.

Hundreds of people attended the funerals of the three boys. They were young, popular and there were many friends and parents of friends and teachers in attendance. Amongst those paying their respects to the grieving family was Frank Whelan.

After the Trail Blazer had disappeared through the guard rail, Frank quickly pulled his small vehicle as far to the right of the road as possible, threw it into park and, with cell phone in hand, ran across the road. As he ran, he dialed nine-one-one, the police emergency number, and apprised the dispatcher of the situation and location. From his position near the ruptured guard rail, he could see the blaze below. He had heard the explosion seconds after the truck went over and knew that the odds were against anyone having survived the blaze, even if they had survived the landing, but he hastily made his way down the slippery, steep embankment anyway, in the hope that someone might have been thrown clear. In the light of the flames, he searched the surrounding area. He found no one. Frank waited, helplessly watching the roaring fire until the police arrived. He gave them all the information he could. Police helicopters had been summoned, but the arrival of police vehicles, ambulances and fire trucks had all been hampered by the muddy roads that led to the scene.

Testing had been done on what was left of the bodies and, through the miracle of modern forensics, it was discovered that all three of the boys' alcohol levels were well above .20.

At the memorial service Frank introduced himself to Jack and Jenny Shikker and offered his condolences. Jack Shikker looked steadily at Frank for a moment, through eyes bloodshot not from alcohol, but from tears. Genuine grief had finally penetrated his wall of anger.

"Do I know you?" Jack asked Frank. "Your name sounds familiar."

Frank was used to this remark. Most people remembered his name from the newspaper accounts of Rachel and Amanda's horrible death.

"No, I don't think so," Frank answered. "I don't believe we've ever met."

"No, I don't think we've met," Jack agreed. "I just know the name."

"Perhaps," Frank repeated gently. He shook hands with Jack and then moved on to say a few words to Jenny. He saw she was pregnant and felt a pang of envy. He thought of Rachel and then shook his head to clear it. He spoke to Jenny mumbling some meaningless phrases, meant to console, but knowing it was like putting a Band-Aid over a ruptured artery. The words offered no real salve. Only time and distance could even begin to offer any possibility of coming to grips with the anguish of losing a child so unexpectedly and so horribly. He knew all this, but could not say any of it. He noticed the little girl beside Jenny. Her face was blotchy from crying. He felt sorry for her. He felt sorry for everyone right now.

# # #

Jack was alone in the house. He was always alone in the house now. He sat at his old kitchen table, each of his hands holding one of his possessions. Around him on the floor were piled thirteen boxes – all the rest of his worldly goods. Tomorrow, this house would belong to someone else.

His father-in-law had sold it out from under him.

Jenny had packed and she and Emily had moved out permanently right after the funeral. They were living with Jenny's parents. And here he sat, jobless and penniless. He shook his head and almost chuckled.

Two newspapers lay open in front of him. One old, giving an account of a young mother who had been ripped asunder by some crazed driver; the other newer and telling the story of three young high school boys who had been the masters of their own fate.

He suddenly had what was probably the most philosophical thought he had ever entertained in his lifetime…

Justice isn't blind. Sometimes, she's just unhurried.

He tipped the beer bottle up with his left hand and finished off the icy liquid savoring the taste. He replaced the bottle gently on the table.

Almost smiling, he lifted his right hand, hefting the burden for a moment before putting the barrel of the .45 caliber pistol in his mouth. He vaguely took notice of the metallic taste as he firmly squeezed the trigger.

THE END

JOE

July 13…

Joe Albruzzi looked up at the faces confronting him. He had been in deep shit before, but never this deep or this dark. Luis Santos, Micky Costanza, Vince Edmond, aka "The Doc," Harry Goldman, and Salvatore "Tiny" Marconi stood on either side gazing down at him as he lay immobilized in the pale blue, satin-lined casket situated in a large viewing room of the funeral home. Save for the six men present, the room was empty of inhabitants. Joe couldn't be sure of the exact time, or the exact day for that matter. He had been drugged and his head felt as if it was filled with wads of prickly cotton balls.

He was pretty sure though, that he was at Randozza's Funeral Parlor located on Nevins Street in downtown Brooklyn. Pauli Randozza was on the family's payroll and he was the most trusted funeral director in the New York area. Especially "sensitive" family matters were usually dealt with through him. Joe knew for a fact that on more than one occasion, two bodies (and sometimes, one body and parts of another) had been laid to rest in the same casket– only one of which was related to the grieving family listed on the board at the main entrance of the funeral home. All of this was accomplished through the cooperation of their kindly funeral director who was well compensated for looking the other way when the family had "business" – meaning the inconvenience of disposing of a body or two.

The lingering smell of flowers pervaded the still air and Joe found himself becoming nauseated by their odor…or perhaps it was the keen awareness of his very short-lived future that was forcing the bile into his belly. He tried to calm himself and hide the fear that was boiling up inside him. He'd seen other men in this same situation – those who knew that their death was imminent. You could see the fear in their eyes, even when they tried to hide it behind a veil of bravado. Their eyes always gave them away. He wondered, in a remote sort of way, what his own dark brown eyes reflected.

Albruzzi had been enjoying a very affluent lifestyle up until a few days ago. He'd had a terrific condo in Manhattan complete with his own personal chef; he employed his own private tailor and hand-rolled cigars made to his specifications were flown in from Cuba every month. Then there were the nightclubs, the limousines and the women. Ah, yes, the women. And, ultimately, that woman whom he had met eight months ago, and who had, unwittingly led him to this moment.

The previous November 5…

He had encountered the woman in question while he was on a business trip in Miami. She worked at the Club Royale and when he saw her on stage, he was hooked. She was a singer there and had the face and the body of an angel, he thought, and he just had to meet her. He signaled the manager to his table and told him to arrange for a meeting after her set. As he shook hands with the man, he slipped him a C-note. The perfectly groomed manager, Marco, secreted the money skillfully without so much as glancing at it, bowed deferentially and delivered the girl to Joe's table personally twenty minutes later. Joe stood as she approached the table. The manager nodded slightly in Joe's direction and discreetly backed away.

She was taller than she appeared on stage, Joe thought.

He was six foot one and she was almost at eye level with him. She offered her hand.

"Hello," he said taking her hand in his. "I know you don't know me, but I really wanted to meet you and to tell you that you have a lovely voice. You're very talented – as well as beautiful. Ahh...where are my manners...I apologize. May I introduce myself? My name is Joe...Joe Albruzzi."

"Thank you. You're so very kind," she replied, guilelessly meeting his admiring gaze. "My name is Ava Lombardi, but you probably already know that."

Joe was pleased to note that her speaking voice was soft and melodious and had only the slightest trace of an East Coast accent. He pulled out a chair and gestured so that she might sit.

"May I offer you a drink?" he asked when they were both seated. "I understand they make a wonderful Manhattan here," he offered.

Thank you, but I'd much prefer a Cosmopolitan, if you don't mind."

"Your wish is my command," replied Joe as he signaled the waiter over to their table.

She leaned back in her chair and crossed her long legs. The uncalculated gesture did not go unnoticed by Joe. The slit in her long, pale pink gown had parted, revealing tanned, well-toned legs ending in ankle-strap, four-inch heels.

"Are you a native Floridian?" he inquired.

"No, I'm originally from New York. I've been here for a little over a year now." she said. She turned slightly and thanked the waiter as he placed her drink in front of her. "I came down after a semester of college. It just wasn't for me. I'm not much of an academic."

She stopped speaking for a moment and looked up at him through lowered lashes. He was watching her intently. She smiled and continued.

"I've always liked warmer weather, so I headed south when I left the City. I was waitressing in a small restaurant when I first arrived, but then my roommate told me that they were looking for chorus girls and singers here. I'm not that great a dancer, but I've always loved to sing. I was in the choir in high school, and I learned to read music there, so I thought I'd give it a try and lo and behold...they hired me."

"And you have your own show now?" Joe asked.

"Their headliner was Marianna Chantelle, but she got married and then got pregnant, so she couldn't work after four months. I'd actually only been here about five months then and management asked me if I'd like to take her place. Who wouldn't? The money's better and I only have to do two shows four nights a week, instead of two shows six nights a week. That was three months ago. I love it here. I love Miami and the Royale and the people. I never want to leave."

"Never?" Joe asked, a smile playing at the corners of his mouth.

"Well, never *is* a long time I guess," Ava admitted smiling.

Ava and Joe were almost inseparable for the next six days, but unexpected pressing business in California suddenly demanded Joe's attention. He'd wanted to pass off the job to an underling, but he knew that this decision would not sit well with his superiors. He was informed that a newcomer was attempting to move in on the business of a very close family friend in San Clemente and Joe was being called in to "discourage" him. A few hasty phone calls secured the muscle he would need for the job. Usually, he would hand-select his men, but he didn't want to spend any more time than necessary to take care of business. He wanted to get back to Miami as soon as possible.

Forty-eight hours after he left, he was back at the Royale in time for Ava's first show of the evening. He knew then that he wanted to have her in his life...preferably forever. This woman had gotten under his skin like no other. He had to talk her into coming back to New York with him. Putting her up in her own place was probably the wisest option, he thought, but he wished he could entice her into moving in with him right away. He did not know how well this would go over with her, however. He had been uncharacteristically patient with her and had not yet gone beyond kissing her good night after their evenings out. He knew without a doubt that she was chaste and he did not want to denigrate her in any way. He was willing to wait for what he wanted – something he had never done before.

Unbeknownst to him, Ava already knew a lot about Joe. She was well aware of his reputation, in both his business and his personal life. He was considered a man-to-be-reckoned-with in both arenas. She had first heard about him when he started his ascent in the ranks. Her grandfather, Figaro Costanza, had been the owner of Vincenzo Olive Products in Brooklyn, but this was only a minor portion of his many business holdings. He had come to the United States from Palermo when he was sixteen and had quickly learned what he had to do in order to secure his future in this new country.

He had begun his career as a youth by running numbers for a small-time operator in Red Hook and had quickly risen up the ranks working for the Calabrese family. His reputation as a ruthless operator grew with time and he became successor to the throne as the powerful and feared don of the "famiglia" when Eduardo Calabrese had a stroke one Sunday morning and was pronounced a vegetable the following Wednesday. Under ordinary circumstances, a Calabrese son would have taken over, but the Calabrese family had suffered a series of unfortunate events that left the infamous don without a male heir.

Figaro went on to make all the right political connections and that, coupled with liberal donations, awarded him the status of an upstanding and respected member of his community who went to church on Sundays with his wife and children and gave generously to charity. His newfound status as a good citizen did not preclude his status as don, however. He continued to mercilessly remove those who stood in his way and ordered whatever disciplinary action necessary to keep in line any waywardly members of his own "family."

Ava was the youngest daughter of Michelangelo Costanza, who was the youngest son of her grandfather. She was well-versed in the ways of the "family" but had come to despise all that they stood for. Her own brothers were being groomed for their places in this world. Anthony, her eldest brother, was attending Oxford. Vincent was at Princeton and John and Nicholas, the twins, were graduating from a private high school next June. She was sure they'd be following Vincent into Princeton. Her sister, Angela, who was the eldest child, had married Edward Marconi and was living on an estate in Colt's Neck, New Jersey with her husband, her three kids (thus far) her staff of housekeepers, gardeners, a chauffeur, two live-in au-pairs, and a chef.

Ava knew the same life was waiting for her with someone whose last name ended in a vowel, but the thought dismayed her. Her mother knew of her daughter's melancholy and she loved this child in a particularly fierce way. Perhaps it was because she reminded her of herself when she was young and full of life and love and high ideals. When Ava came to her one night about year ago, Francine Costanza gave her almost all the money she had secreted away since she'd been married to Michelangelo and helped her slip out from under the watchful eyes of the family and the household staff. It was a dangerous move for both of them, but she knew that her daughter would never escape her "destiny" if she didn't get away and she knew too that her child's high spirit would wither and die if she was subjected to the life she was fated to live.

When Ava had first seen Joe she thought he had been sent to bring her back but, apparently, he did not recognize her. She'd considered running once again while he was on his trip to California, but then decided against it. He had affected her in ways she would never have expected. She had heard stories of how charming he was and how women would fall all over him, and she had no doubts that all or almost all of these stories were based in facts.

What had held her in place was that she thought she

had discovered another side of this man. Of course, she had originally found him appealing enough. After all, he *was* handsome in an Italian, Cary Grant sort of way and wealthy and he *did* have a quirky sense of humor and he *was* amazingly respectful of her – a trait she had never associated with his reputation. Even after knowing who he was though, she couldn't help but be fascinated. She had tapped into something else…a part of him that she believed he didn't allow too many people to know…perhaps, no one was *ever* allowed to know. In their long talks into the evening, she had discovered that he was enduring and sensitive and was himself not all that happy about the life he was leading. He was, of course, lured by the things that money could provide for him, but there was a part of him, (grant you, a very small part, but it *was* still there), which was saddened by the man he had become. This tiny fraction of his persona was what had allowed her to drop her guard and now she felt herself being drawn inexorably back into the life she deplored. She was falling in love with Joe.

He presented her with diamond earrings on the Saturday night after his return from California and then added the matching bracelet on Sunday and the matching necklace on the following Saturday. She was quietly pleased, but hastened to tell Joe that the baubles weren't necessary…they were beautiful, but not necessary to convince her that she wanted to be with him. However, she was still very reluctant to leave Miami. Joe couldn't understand why.

"It's not good for me," she told him. "I...I don't like the cold weather and it's...dangerous."

"Dangerous?" Joe questioned, raising an eyebrow.

"Yes, well, perhaps dangerous is too strong a word. It's not good for my career. I mean, if I catch a cold, it could ruin my voice, and...and I don't know if I could do as well in a big city," she hastily explained.

"Oh, *that* kind of dangerous," Joe laughed. "You sounded so darkly intriguing for a moment. Anyway, I know a lot of people in the entertainment business. Some of them owe me 'favors.' I know they would be willing to place you in a show...or even headline you. Once they've heard you sing, they'll feel they *still* owe me a favor."

"No!" she exclaimed, almost vehemently, tossing her head so that her dark hair fell over her eyes. She raked her fingers through it impatiently. "I don't want...what I mean is, I appreciate your help, Joe, but I need to do it on my own. You can understand that, can't you?" Ava searched Joe's eyes. "I want to be with you Joe. But, I really think I'm better off here...for a while, anyway."

Joe smiled his most charming smile and he could see Ava's defenses weakening. He had that effect on most women. He was thirty-one years old and movie star handsome. Had he attempted a Hollywood career, he was sure he could have made a go of it just on his looks, but memorizing all those lines would be a bore. He'd rather make up his own life story as he went along. The lifestyle/career he had chosen was perilous, but it paid well – very well, in fact, and he was moving up the ranks very quickly. He had originally liked the whole idea of living life on the edge, and had fast become addicted to the power it offered. But somewhere inside, something was missing, and he was beginning to question his career choice – admittedly a dangerous question.

He knew that originally, he had desired Ava because of her looks and her body. That had always been his criteria. But very quickly, he had found himself enchanted by this lovely young woman with the haunting green eyes and the delicate hands that fluttered like butterflies when she spoke. He liked talking with her. She had a lot to say and was wiser than her years, but she listened to him too...*really listened...* and asked questions of him that no one had ever asked. She probed deep into his psyche and he found his defenses falling away...and, he liked it.

In turn, Ava knew in her heart that she should tell Joe about herself...*everything* about herself, but she feared that if she did, she would lose him – perhaps forever – and she did not want to risk that fate. She decided to wait to tell him...for a little while longer, at least. She thought she could stall the trip north for a few months anyway, and she knew that if she could hold out for eleven months, all would be well. She had answered all the questions he had posed to her about her life…she had just omitted a few of the baser details.

It took Joe four subsequent trips to Miami over the next five months to convince Ava that he was indeed serious about their relationship. Subtle inquiries Joe made around Miami after his return from California reinforced the background story that Ava had given him. Inquiries in the New York area led to a dead end. No one had ever heard of Ava Lombardi but, of course, that meant nothing. Theoretically, it only meant that she had no family ties. She had already told him that she was estranged from her family and that most of them no longer lived in New York, which was a true fact. With her brothers all away at school and her sister and her parents in New Jersey, New York was pretty much free of her family.

Amongst the minutia she had omitted from the stories she told about herself, was the fact that Lombardi was not her real family name. She had taken her mother's maiden name as her own when she fled to Florida. One other piece of information had also been fabricated. Neither Joe nor her employer were aware that she was only seventeen years old. She'd been just sixteen when she'd begun her career.

July 6…

They say everyone has a twin somewhere in the world, and that was what John Romano thought when he saw Ava singing at the Blue Parrott Club in Greenwich Village in New York City that night. Her hair was different than he remembered when he'd met Ava Costanza two or three years ago, and she was billed as Ava Lombardi and she looked to be about twenty-five or six. And, of course, Ava had never been a singer that he knew of, but still…he scratched his chin thoughtfully…she sure could pass for Ava. He was still thinking about it that night when he stopped at the Tavern on the Green for a late night supper. As luck would have it, he ran into Jerry Roscoe and his girl who were also having a late night meal after having gone to a Broadway show. When Jerry spotted John, he called to him, inviting John to join them.

As it turned out Jerry's date was Susan Goldman, Harry Goldman's sister, a vacant bleached blonde with a new nose too small and too pert for her broad face. When John casually mentioned the singer with the uncanny resemblance to Ava, Susan, who had been staring blankly into space, perked up with sudden interest.

"The family's still lookin' fer her, ya know," she said in her pronounced nasal, Brooklyn accent. "An', there's a reward fer whoever finds her…a hundred thousan' dollars (she pronounced this last word 'dallahs')…no questions asked. It probably isn't her, but ya never know. I'll tawk to my brotha."

And that was how Joe ended up lying in this particular casket, mouth, hands and feet securely bound with duct tape. He had just been given a brief synopsis of the story by Harry. The rest had watched with varying degrees of anger and disgust etched on their faces. He wanted very much to tell Harry and Mickey and everyone else present that he hadn't known. He hadn't known that she was Mickey's daughter and for sure he hadn't known that she wasn't even eighteen years old! He wanted to scream at them and tell them that his intentions had been honorable, and that he loved her and had intended to marry her, but he wasn't going to get a chance to say anything apparently, because as he looked up from his horizontal prison the coffin lid was closed and he heard the lock tumble firmly into place.

July 29…

"This is CNN reporter David Jones coming to you live from Croton-on-the-Hudson in New York. I'm standing on the private dock of homeowner Brenda Dietz where, just an hour and forty minutes ago, a casket was found floating next to Ms. Dietz' catamaran." The reporter turned swiftly from

Camera One to face the beleaguered woman. "Ms. Dietz, could you tell us what happened here today, please?"

Brenda, a thirty-something divorcee, looked shyly into the camera and pulled back perceptibly from the microphone that had been thrust into her face by the CNN reporter. She glanced at him with alarm. He withdrew the mike a few inches and smiled at her encouragingly.

"It's all right, Brenda. Just tell the folks what you told me earlier. You can just talk to me if you'd like."

Jones was seasoned enough to know that not everyone did well with mikes and cameras pointing into their faces, and this woman had been sufficiently shaken by her discovery of the day, and then by the telling and re-telling of her story to the authorities. She didn't need to be terrified into silence by the mikes and cameras. Better that should happen on someone else's interview, he thought. She turned to him hesitantly and began her story, not even aware that one of the cameramen had inconspicuously made his way behind the reporter and was shooting his footage from there.

"Well," she began, "I usually go out on the boat early in the morning, but I had some things to attend to today, so I was delayed. As I was coming down here, I heard a knocking sound, but I thought it was one of my neighbors doing repairs on his dock. Sometimes, it's hard to tell the direction a sound is coming from when you're near the water. Anyway, when I got down here, the banging was louder and I started looking around to see what it was and then I looked behind the boat. This…casket…was floating and banging up against the back of my boat. It had gotten caught between the boat and the grasses. It was low tide, so I guess it was caught on the bottom too. I didn't recognize it for what it was right away. I mean, who expects to find a coffin floating in the river, right? Well, I had my cell phone in my pocket…I never go out on the river without it…and I called nine-one-one right away, and…that's about it."

"Could you tell us about what time that was, Brenda?"

"Oh, sure," Brenda replied. "It was exactly eleven twenty-nine. I know because I looked at my phone before I made the call."

"Thank you so much for your time, Brenda." Jones was already turning to Camera Two in front of him, which was now focusing in on his appropriately somber face.

"The police have not yet identified the body that was found within the casket, nor have they released any particulars concerning the death, but we have been told that the body is that of a male. Details are being withheld pending investigation and notification of family members.

"We hope to have more information on this developing story later in the day, and we will keep you up-to-date as we do. This is David Jones, CNN News from Croton-on-the-Hudson."

August 4…

Ava Costanza sat in the parlor of her parent's home in Berkley Heights, New Jersey, TV remote held listlessly in her right hand. The TV was on, but she was neither watching nor listening. Instead, she was thinking of Joe and trying to decide if she should be angry with him or frightened for him or both. It was almost three weeks since she seen him.

Joe had finally talked Ava into leaving Florida with the promise of an audition and an apartment – both available the minute she decided to move to New York. Ava was reluctant, but she wanted to see Joe more often than once every few weeks and so had gone against what her sensibilities had dictated.

She smiled inwardly when she remembered how excited he had been when she told him of her decision to go.

"Remember, Ava, this will be only an audition. I mean, I know you said you want to make it on your own and all, so the only strings I pulled were to get you the audition at this new club a friend of mine opened a few months ago. It's called the Blue Parrott and it's in Greenwich Village. And I took the liberty of securing an apartment for you that's only a few blocks away. It's in a brownstone and you'll have the parlor floor and the top floor to yourself."

Ava began protesting, thinking what the rent on a place like that must cost.

Joe had placed a finger gently over her lips.

"Nuh uh, I don't want to hear it. I own that brownstone. Bought it as an investment about three years ago. The tenants who were there had a two-year lease and they decided to move uptown, so that left me with an empty apartment as of four weeks ago. It's not good to have an empty apartment. Makes the downstairs tenants nervous.

"Anyway, you can use it for as long as you like; you can pay me rent once you get a job and start making money if you want, but until then, it's yours. The only reason I'll accept for you not moving in there is if you don't like the place…but I don't think that's going to happen. Oh, did I tell you there's a courtyard garden with a private entrance that's part of the deal?"

Ava had laughed at this. She had told him, when they first met that one of the things she didn't like about her apartment in Florida was not having access to the outside once she got home.

"I'd love to be able to go home and sit out under the stars at night or be able to take my breakfast or lunch out to my own garden, but I'm lucky if I can find a place to stand in my galley kitchen and shove in a bowl of cornflakes."

After having seen her apartment, Joe knew what she meant. He couldn't understand how she could live in such a confined space. Aside from the galley kitchen there was a small living room with a narrow couch that opened out into a bed. Period. The whole place was probably no more than two hundred and fifty square feet, including the miniscule bathroom. He'd made a convincing argument and Ava had made a decision that would change the course of her life and seriously alter Joe's.

Ava had gone north to Manhattan on her audition and had won over both the owner and his small band. He told her that the Club would be ready for its new show in about six weeks. He hadn't changed anything since he took over, but now that things were running smoothly, he thought the time was right to put on a new show with new entertainers. He wanted to know if she would be able to start rehearsals when they were ready. Ava was flying high. She couldn't believe she had actually gotten a job in New York City! Of course Joe had opened the door for her, but she had made it and that's what counted.

That had been such a short time ago, but it had amounted to almost a lifetime, she thought wryly.

Ava had been anxious about leaving Florida. So anxious in fact, that she had packed and then unpacked her suitcases twice. She knew she loved Joe , and she was sure that he loved her in return. In the time they'd spent together, she'd learned that he was basically a good man who had made some very unwise choices. He'd confided in her that he was ready to start life anew with her in a place where neither of them had ties. He had to finish up business in New York first…tie up some loose ends. Completing this would probably take about a year, he'd told her. But then…

He had saved enough money, he said, so that they could get married and move west – somewhere like Colorado or Montana – perhaps buy a house or maybe even a small ranch. They could raise sheep or horses or cows and…children. Lots of children, Joe had emphasized. Ava had melted into this idea. She could see herself and Joe in a big, warm kitchen that had French doors that opened onto a spacious patio with a path that led to the garden where on the lawn there were swing sets for the children, and beyond that open pastures with beautiful horses and beyond that, mountain ranges whose tops were lost in snow and blue sky. Ava packed her small treasury of costumes and clothing and never looked back.

That first month in New York had been like a dream. During the first three weeks, her days were spent in long but exciting rehearsals at the Blue Parrott. Her nights were spent with Joe. He would arrive in her apartment around seven and either bring dinner or they'd prepare dinner together and then…they would talk. Almost every evening they would decide, while having dinner, that they should go to a movie or go dancing or take a walk in the park. By the time dinner was over however, they'd be deep in conversation and be loath to interrupt it to go anywhere. And so they'd curl up on the big, soft couch, she with her hot chocolate and he with his demitasse…and as the evenings passed, their spirits entwined in an ever-tightening circle.

She returned to the present with a start. Joe…*her* Joe was on TV. Not him actually – his picture. What was his picture doing on TV? She lifted the remote and aimed it at the TV screen.

"…days in the water. As you may remember, the grisly discovery was made last week by a woman who was preparing to take her catamaran out onto the Hudson River. Authorities are not releasing any further information, but it is widely alleged that Albruzzi was a member of the Scalia crime family. Whether this misdeed was the work of a rival family or the Scalia's own handiwork has not yet been established, and indeed, may never be.

"This is Charles Hurley reporting to you from the Dorado Street precinct, Croton-on-the-Hudson."

Ava sat deathly still, eyes wide and dilated. Her arm, which she had held stiffly out in front of her, had dropped limply to her side, loosening her grip on the remote control. It dropped silently onto the thick ivory carpet. This is what it feels like to die, she thought. Total nothing as far as the eye could see…no feelings…no hope…just an ineffable void.

# # #

Joe sat on a white folding chair in the hallway of what apparently was a hospital. He was wearing a navy blue pinstripe suit, a white linen shirt, a steel blue tie and his favorite wingtips, and he had no idea why he was here, or for that matter, how he had arrived. Come to think of it, he didn't even know where "here" was. A feeling of foreboding overtook him, leading to a bizarre reaction of overpowering vertigo. Not a common, everyday lightheadedness – actual vertigo – as if he were Alice falling headlong down the rabbit hole – powerless to stop himself.

This was not the Joe Albruzzi he knew. The Joe Albruzzi he knew would stand and fight – not curl up and tremble like a little girl. Something was happening here. Something he did not understand at all. He dropped his lead low between his knees, hoping to quell the roiling in his stomach that was now accompanying the giddiness.

"That's right. Just try and take it easy for now. Keep that head of yours down for a minute or two. The wooziness will pass soon enough. Just about everyone gets that way at first."

Joe managed a few deep breaths as he stared at the

tips of well-worn but clean tan top-siders that were in his line of vision as he was bent over. He took a deep breath, closed his eyes and slowly raised his head. He opened his eyes and found himself looking at a tall man dressed in a white polo shirt, tan chinos and a Mets baseball cap. What appeared to be a silk baseball jacket was slung casually over his left shoulder, held in place by his left forefinger. He extended his right hand towards Joe.

"Moses," he said simply.

"Excuse me?" Joe said.

"My name, son. Moses. Moses Samuel Davis, to be precise."

"Oh, sorry," Joe mumbled by way of apology. He stood and extended his own hand. "Joe Albruzzi."

"New here, eh?" inquired Moses.

"I...I guess so," Joe replied hesitantly. "Uh...could you...well, I...OK." Joe took another deep breath as he stood, and brought his head up to face the other man. "This might sound crazy to you but I don't know where I am, exactly," he finally said.

Moses looked at him kindly.

"That's OK, son. Very few know where they are initially. It's only natural. What's the last thing you remember?"

Joe's eyes slid out of focus as he struggled to

remember anything at all. Suddenly a jolt, not unlike a bolt of electricity shot through him as he remembered the pale blue satin lining of a casket being lowered in place over him as he watched helplessly.

"Oh, my God."

Joe felt his legs turn to rubber as all his memories flooded back to him, tumbling over each other in their effort to rush into their proper timeline.

"It's all right, Joe. Just sit down until it passes. That rush of last memory is usually so strong it comes at you like a sucker punch in the gut."

"Oh, my God," Joe repeated, in a whisper more reverent now than surprised.

"Yup. You got it, son. Here, He's generally referred to as The Boss." Moses said.

Joe felt as if he had gotten on the biggest, highest roller coaster ever made, but it had no visible means of support and it sped faster and faster still until even its tracks were lost in the blur of speed and – best of all – he had no way of getting off! His head began to spin once again.

"Mmm..." Moses observed with a grin. "The old roller coaster analogy, eh?"

Joe stared at Moses for a beat.

"Everyone here can read everyone else's thoughts. We don't generally exercise that particular ability – a matter of courtesy you understand – but we're all capable. I find it helps sometimes with newcomers to dig in and find out what's going on in there. Helps the transition process go a bit easier."

"But I," Joe began...

"I know. You can't read my thoughts. That's because it takes a bit of time for the process to kick in. Kind of a safety feature. If you could do it from the get-go, it would make things a lot more complicated for you. You wouldn't know what you were hearing from whom, or how to shut it off and you couldn't focus on the business at hand, so to speak.

"Now, don't worry about it. It's nothing for you to be concerned with right now. Right now, we have more important matters to discuss."

Joe nodded his head automatically, even though he still wasn't in tune with his situation. He was trying his hardest to concentrate. One of the things that had made him as successful as he was in business was listening and fully assessing situations rather than leaping to conclusions without full insight, although he was finding that particular feat progressively more difficult.

"That's right, Joe. That mode of thinking is always the way to go. If more people evaluated their situations more thoroughly, there'd be a lot less disputes on Earth...a lot less good men lost to wars and common street fighting."

Joe opened his mouth to speak, thought better of it and

snapped it shut, feeling as if his soul had been laid bare. He guessed it pretty much had.

Seven months later…

Ava brought a cup of black coffee over to table number four. The old man in the pork pie hat looked up at her and smiled thinly by way of saying 'thank you'. She turned and walked back behind the diner's counter without acknowledging him. The old man was named Boomer – not his real name, of course. She had known him for most of her life as "Uncle Boomer," and he was one of the lesser enforcers in the Costanza family. He was now around seventy-five years old she guessed, and long since retired. Retired or not, he had been called in by her father…to baby-sit. He was one of five, around-the-clock guardians who followed her every move – every day, every moment of her life since she had been discovered that fateful evening at the Blue Parrott.

A part of her – the part of herself that she suspected was her soul – had died the day she heard the news about Joe. His murderers had never been found, but she knew in her heart that at least one of them had been her father. When she had finally shaken the paralysis of mind that had suffused her the day she had heard about Joe's death, she had gone to her father, not screaming as she had wanted to, but deadly calm.

She told him that she was going to attend Joe's funeral. When he began to object, she cut him off, countering with two arguments he could not dispute. She told him that if he did not let her go, she would find a way to end her own life. If that option did not present itself in a timely fashion, she would retreat so far into herself, that death would be preferable to all those around her. Either way, he would lose her forever. Michelangelo Costanza, a powerful man used to getting his own way, yielded.

Ava knew that her father had guards watching her, but she led a life now that simply marked time. No cars, taxis, trips, theaters…no more singing. She stayed in her room – making it her self-imposed prison – and left only to go to work or to sit on the private veranda just outside her room. The door to her room was never locked. It didn't have to be. Ava had retreated within herself, allowing no one entry.

Knowing her father wanted her to return to school, she refused. She preferred to work as a waitress at the Galaxy Diner. Part of its charm was that she could walk there from where she stayed. She would no longer use the word "home" when referring to the well-appointed bedroom suite she was forced to occupy in her father's house. The uncomplicated tasks of the job she had chosen grounded her and kept her sane.

She knew that her father wanted her to marry. She

would not. She told him one night, as he was extolling the virtues of marrying a suitor he had chosen for her that she was going to die a virgin so that when she went to Heaven, she would be able to be together with Joe and he would know that she was as pure as when they had last met. Her father's usually unreadable dark eyes were filled with disbelief.

"That's right, Daddy dear. I am still a virgin. You want me to go to a Doctor to prove it to you? I will, you know. Joe never touched me. He wanted to marry me. He had respect for me…more respect for me than you will ever have."

Michelangelo Costanza's eyes now burned with fury and he did something he had never before done in his life. He slapped his daughter across the face with such force that she staggered back, grabbing onto the back of a chaise to avoid falling.

Ava righted herself and simply smiled serenely at him, turned and walked out of the room. She never spoke to her father directly again.

# # #

Joe sat listening to Moses for a very long time. Moses recounted stories that Joe remembered hearing from his mother when he was a little boy. He felt a tug of nostalgia in his heart for those days that were so relatively effortless. When he thought of those times spent with his mother and father, he felt as if he had been in a cocoon filled with warm sunshine and the smells of his mother's Chantilly Lace perfume and his father's Old Spice cologne. Just the thought of those days flooded his senses. The thing of it was, he couldn't remember when that nice kid left and the tough, would-be wise-guy emerged.

He was no longer sitting in a white folding chair in a hospital corridor. He was now sitting on a white Adirondack chair on a white porch, overlooking a meadow of lush wildflowers. A cool breeze made the flowers sway like ocean waves and their scent floated across to him sweet and inviting. The sky was the clearest azure blue he had ever seen and the sun dazzling. He held a glass of icy lemonade in his left hand. Joe had no recollection of how he came to be on this porch, holding this lemonade. As he stared at the glass, he remembered that his mom's fresh lemonade had been his favorite as a child, and this tasted suspiciously like it. He was, however, beginning to accept that unusual things were not quite so unusual here.

"You do have certain options, Joe."

Joe looked up. "Options?" he repeated.

"Well, yes. You see, you were actually taken before you were scheduled. That happens once in a great while. You left…'unfinished business' I think is the popular phrase. Your leaving was…unjust and untimely. Your intentions with Ava were genuinely honorable because for the first time in your life, you were sincerely in love. Ava is a very good person and an excellent judge of character, Joe. She loved you almost from the beginning, even though she knew who you were."

Joe looked up in surprise. This was the first time he and Moses had touched upon his involvement with Ava. "What do you mean, she knew who I was."

"Joe, there was something you never knew about Ava. She wanted no more involvement with her family or their way of life. That was why she was so hesitant about returning to New York. Ava never told you that she'd run away from home – with her mother's blessing, by the way – because she abhorred involving you. Then, she was just afraid to tell you, although I know she was planning on it.

"She used her mother's maiden name when she fled to Florida. Ava's father wanted her back because his pride would not let him believe that a child of his would not want to be involved in the family, but also because no one was allowed to have something that was his, without his consent. He didn't know if she'd gone off alone or with someone, but he put out a reward for her 'capture' – as if she were a wayward prisoner. He didn't use that word, but it was implied.

"She knew who you were more or less from day one. However, you intrigued her, even though she knew of your reputation. You offered her a part of yourself that you tried very hard to suppress in other parts of your life. That was the man she fell in love with. Perhaps if she had told you earlier who she was, it might have saved you, although I doubt it. More likely, it would have caused more deaths and your soul would have been blackened by them."

Joe lowered his head, shame flooding him. "I led a really bad life," he said.

"Well, yes and no," Moses said slowly. "Your life was not exactly exemplary, but your soul...well, your soul was never truly corrupt. You wanted the good life and you side-stepped the straight and narrow to get it, but you also did things that, had they been known by your superiors, would definitely have been frowned upon, to put it mildly."

"I wish I hadn't been...well, who I was. Then, I wouldn't be here now."

"Well, again, perhaps yes and perhaps no. Keep in mind Joe that your life impacts many others...even those you are not aware of or who are not aware of you. For example, do you remember a man by the name of Cortez? Vittorio Cortez?"

"No, I...oh, wait...yeah...Vic. Liked the ponies a little too much, but he was a pretty good guy. Whatever happened to him?"

"Do you remember the circumstances that led up to your meeting him Joe?"

"Yeah...I remember. Eddie Scalia wanted me to break

his kneecaps because Vic owed him money. The thing of it was, when I tracked Vic down, he was working in a grocery store and moonlighting at the downtown Lowe's Cinema. I was alone on the job and I'd muscled him out to the alley behind the movie theater with every intention of carrying out Eddie's orders. It was the first year I was working for Eddie. I was tryin' to 'make my bones,' as they say. Anyway, I get him back there, and I tell him Eddie sent me so now he knows why I'm there. And you know, he didn't beg or bawl about it. He owns up and says 'yeah, I know I owe him. That's why I'm workin' two jobs...so's I can pay him back. I know you're just doin' your job here, but could I ask you somethin' please?'

"I say 'what'? I kinda snarled it, because I'm still playing the tough enforcer and I'm not taking any crap from anyone. Anyway, he tells me his wife is expecting and could I please break his arm or something so he can still go to work and have the medical insurance to pay for his wife to have the baby, so they don't have to go on welfare or anything. Plus, this way, he can still pay back the dough he owes Eddie. Now, I'm floored! I ask him how much he's into Eddie for. He tells me he owes fifteen hundred. I just looked at him. 'Fifteen hundred'? I asked. 'Yeah,' he says. I'd never asked Eddie how much the guy owed, because it wasn't my business. But I know fifteen hundred is nothing to Eddie. The guy drops that much when he takes his buddies out barhopping! And I guess what got me most of all was…this guy, Vic…there's a…dignity, I guess would be the right word…yeah, dignity…there's a dignity about him. I mean, I've got him dead to rights…he admits he owes the dough and he's behind in his payments and he knows I can carry out Eddie's orders and he's willing to take his punishment…but he's talking to me quietly and politely. I mean he's scared, but he's not groveling. It just got to me, so I made him a deal. I told him that I would pay Eddie and tell Eddie that *he* gave me the dough. Now, he owes *me*, but I tell him that as long as he keeps paying me a little something every week, I won't bother him. Of course, I also told him that if I got word that anyone else knew of our deal, the deal would be off, and I'd do more than Eddie had ordered me to do. You understand, I still had to be tough…or it wouldn't work. I told him to stay away from the ponies and stay home with his wife and new kid. He told me he was already going for help with his problem and that he was indebted to me for my kindness. He said that if there was ever anything I could do for him, even though he doubted it, I should just call on him. Then he shook my hand."

"And, did he keep his word?"

"You know he did! It took him a little over a year, but he paid me off."

"Do you know what happened to him after that?"

Moses asked.

"Funny thing," Joe replied. "I kinda lost track of him after he finished paying me."

"He became a firefighter, Joe. He became a firefighter because he liked helping people and because he discovered it was the best way he could support his family. His wife gave birth to twins you know, about ten days after your little talk with him."

"Yeah? Nice…" Joe mused.

"Anyway, about a year after he became a firefighter, he was off-duty when a fire broke out in a house that he passed every day on his way to work. He was on his way home one night, saw the fire, called it in and then ran in to help. He saved a mother and her three children that day. Managed to save the family dog too.

"So you see Joe, if you'd never become a 'wise-guy' all those lives would be very different than they are because you wouldn't have been the one sent to coerce Vic into submission. And if you'd carried out Eddie's orders and had not used your heart, Vic and his wife would probably have raised their children in poverty and that mother and her three children might not have survived that day. Remember, Joe, everything happens for a reason though we may not understand it, and we touch many others on our journey through life.

"There were a few other incidents too, Joe. Times that you wanted to be the big, bad wolf but managed to play a sort of guardian angel to a few, misguided souls. You see *here*, good deeds never go *un*rewarded."

Joe shook his head in amazement. "Wow…" was all he could summon up.

"Anyway, back to the *options* we need to discuss."

"Yeah," Joe said. "*That* really has my interest!"

"Now you know, Joe that you can never go back…at least, not entirely."

Joe looked at Moses perplexed. "Entirely…what does that mean, exactly?" he questioned.

"Let me explain," Moses continued. "If you went back as Joe Albruzzi people would tend to stare, the police would be baffled, people you know would be…horrified."

Joe smirked thinking about the reaction of Eddie and Santos and the Doc and Marconi and especially Micky Costanza. Those guys would probably have a heart attack, he thought.

"I think they'd try and kill me again," he finally admitted to Moses. "I think they'd just do it again."

"You're right, Joe. They would. But…now hear me out on this one. What if your 'brother' suddenly showed up? Your brother who's an attorney, let's say. And he has a legal document, signed by you that he'd been holding onto which you'd given him in the event of your untimely death. And, let's just say for arguments sake that this document has lots of numbers and dates and incidents in it. The kind of numbers and dates and incidents that could make things rather sticky for a few people. The kind that would you allow you certain 'privileges' and a certain amount of protection from those same people."

"Well, that might work," Joe admitted. "However, the families all knew that I was an only child and that my parents were long gone and that I had…no one."

"Just think about it for a moment, Joe. In your business, is everyone exactly forthcoming? Who's to say that you just said that you had no family of your own in order to protect them, or that maybe they disowned you when they discovered which path you had chosen in your life, or that you had simply walked out of their lives?"

Joe hesitated and then spoke.

"Is it possible? Do you think it would work? I mean, *how* would it work? Would I just go back and say I am my twin?"

"No, Joe. It doesn't work like that. *You* per se don't get to go back. Your spirit, the essence of your soul is what gets to go back and it will inhabit the body of someone whose time on Earth has ended. It will be someone who fits the general physical and geographical requirements and I think my original idea of an attorney would work to our advantage. It would have to be someone who has enough legal connections of his own to give him clout. Let's face it, if he enters the picture waving a piece of paper around and threatening the family's security, he would be in serious jeopardy and we'll be having this conversation yet again and much sooner than later."

"Hell, yeah," Joe agreed. His face flushed.

Moses grinned. "Don't worry, son. We don't expect you to grow wings overnight. But we do expect something in return. You're getting a second chance here and we'd like to see you do something with it. Agreed?"

Joe took the proffered hand.

"Agreed," he said.

# # #

April 16…

Michael Richard Lambrusco surveyed the contents of his briefcase. Everything seemed to be in order. He carefully closed and locked it, glancing at his watch as he grabbed at his overnight bag. Late, as usual. He felt a fleeting surge of annoyance with himself because he'd spent so much time this afternoon in the conference room, meeting with the senior partner, even though he knew he had a six o'clock flight to

Chicago. But, on the upside, Hillman Devon, the senior partner in the firm of Fields, Devon and McDougal had made rather loud noises inferring that Lambrusco was being closely regarded by Fields and Devon and was in line for the next partnership. That was something that Lambrusco was not willing to pass up – even if it *did* mean running for a flight. It certainly wasn't the first time, he thought as he hailed the cab on Lexington Avenue.

"Kennedy Airport," he fairly shouted at the driver as he hustled himself into the back seat. "And hurry, please!" he added. "I'm late for my flight!"

"I will do my very best for you, sir," the driver replied in a voice thick with an undetermined accent. "You see though that we are nearing the rush hour, and it will not be easy."

"I know, I know," Michael replied. "There's an extra twenty in it for you if you can get me there in forty-five minutes."

"I do not think Allah himself could get you there in forty-five minutes," the driver mumbled under his breath. To Michael, he said, "As I said, sir, I will do my best for you."

Michael's teeth rattled as the taxi's rear tire slammed into a pothole as it made a left off Lexington and headed towards East River Drive. He cursed mildly to himself, popped an antacid into his mouth and tightened his seat belt.

April 18…

Ava regarded the palm tree that stood in a vast ceramic pot in the corner of the patio. The graceful fronds swayed gently in the wind. If she focused on it hard enough, she thought, she could block out all her other surroundings and pretend she was back in Florida, back before death and all its horror had entered her life.

She started as she heard a sound from behind her, and turned to see her mother standing in the doorway that led to her room.

"I'm glad to see you out there. You should be outdoors on such a lovely day. You're so pale my little girl. The sun will do you good."

"I hadn't noticed," Ava said, referring to the loveliness of the day. "I just came out to…think. It's so much easier when all there is to look at is grass and trees."

Ava's mother scrutinized her daughter. She had probably lost twenty pounds in the past year or so she thought. Her skin was so pale as to be almost transparent. Miraculously, her long dark hair had lost none of its luster, but it seemed to be too much of a burden for her slender neck. 'Wispy' was the word that came to the forefront of Francine Costanza's thoughts when describing her youngest child. She looked as though she was simply fading away.

April 20…

Michael Lambrusco was staring up at the cantilevered ceiling of O'Hare Airport. There were people milling around him, many of them shouting, but he barely heard them. And, he noted, he was beginning to lose sight of them too. He closed his eyes in an effort to concentrate on how he came to be lying on the floor of the concourse of the airport.

He'd had his final meeting with the corporate attorneys at the offices of RMC, Inc. and despite his trepidation, all had gone quite smoothly. The meeting had run a bit over scheduled time, but not much. He'd hailed a cab and they'd headed straight for O'Hare. Oh, of course, he thought. There'd been an accident – not involving him, but an accident nevertheless that had backed up traffic for over forty minutes and he'd arrived at the airport fifteen minutes before departure. He was racing through the concourse, heading for his gate when he'd felt the first signs of indigestion. As he was running, he reached into his pocket, grabbed an antacid and was about to pop it into his mouth when he tripped. Wait…no…he didn't trip. He'd started seeing these stars…almost like miniature flashbulbs popping in front of his eyes. He'd slowed his pace a bit and then he'd started sweating and then he'd gone down – almost in slow motion. Gone down and now could not find the strength to get up again. OK…he'd lie here for a moment with his eyes closed, and then he'd be fine…just fine…His chest heaved with his effort to draw in air.

# # #

"There's someone now, Joe. He's an attorney of Italian descent, young…twenty-nine years old, nice looking fella too. He's about three months away from making partner in a very prestigious law firm in Manhattan. He's doing very well. So well that he's never taken the time to eat right or relax or have any kind of social life. He's been practically inhaling antacids for almost a year now for his constant indigestion…except that it's not indigestion."

"He has a bad ticker?" Joe asked, the anxiety clear in his voice.

"Yes. But not something that can't be reversed by some real lifestyle changes. Life is not meant to be lived at break-neck speed, Joe. It's meant to be enjoyed and savored. Most people have gotten to the point where all they savor is fine wine or fine foods. That's all very well and good, but that's not all there is. There are so many wonderful gadgets that have been invented to save people precious time…but where is all that saved time going?

"Joe, Michael's time is up and he'll soon join us here, and you have the opportunity to take over where he left off. It's your decision."

Joe took a deep breath. "Whoa," was all he could manage.

"Time is of the essence, Joe. If we don't move quickly, this opportunity will slide by and I don't know when the next one will present itself. As I explained to you before, you'll have all the information you need to carry out what needs to be done. In time, any memory of your time here and of Joe – the Joe you are now – will fade, and you'll be able to carry on your life as Michael. Your memories of Joe will be as they should be…as that of a brother. But, what you choose to do with your life as Michael will remain your decision.

"Son, I just hope you've learned enough here to affect your time on Earth. Time is the most precious commodity in the world…not money nor power nor fame. And it's what we do with the time we have that defines our life.

"Now, do you think you're ready?"

Joe looked Moses squarely in the eye. "I am," he said.

# # #

Joe experienced a feeling of lightheadedness as he passed through a blur of color and then gasped as a bolus of electric passed through his body, forcing his back to arch. His eyelids fluttered and he found himself gazing into the concerned faces of three EMTs.

"Hey there, welcome back," one said. "How're you feeling, Mr. Lambrusco?"

"Lambrusco?" Joe whispered hoarsely after a pause.

"It's OK, sir," said another. "Just lay there and take a minute and breathe naturally. You've had a coronary episode. You're hooked up with an oxygen mask to make it easier for you to breathe and there's an IV in your arm. We're going to put you on a gurney and get you into the ambulance in a few moments. We wanted to stabilize you before transporting you to the hospital. Try not to worry, you're doing just fine. We going to take you to Lutheran General and they'll finish checking you out there."

"OK," Joe (now Michael) said weakly. His eyes felt too heavy to keep open, but suddenly he remembered something. He lifted his oxygen mask off his face. "Please, would you mind making sure I have my briefcase? I have a lot of important stuff in there."

"Sure, sure," said EMT number three slipping the mask back down. "Don't you worry about anything now. We have your briefcase and your carry-on. Your wallet is inside your carry-on. We pulled it from your jacket to look for ID."

"OK, fine." Michael replied. He lifted the mask again. "I just wanted to say 'thanks' in case I forget later…thanks for everything you did."

"Thanks for coming back," EMT number three said, replacing the mask once again. "You made our day!"

"OK, guys," he called to the others. "Let's get him

outta here!"

April 25...

Michael stepped into a cab that was waiting in line at the airport. He gave the driver the address that was on his driver's license. He took a deep breath as he relaxed against the back seat of the taxi. Physically, he felt ok. He felt a little weaker than he was used to feeling as Joe, but not too bad. The Doctors in Chicago had discharged him early this morning with a bottle of pills and a list of New York cardiologists. He'd taken the earliest flight possible out of O'Hare into Kennedy. He wanted very much to begin his new life.

Tossing his keys on the half round table in the entrance hall, he looked around the condo that was now his. It was located in a brownstone on the Upper East Side of Manhattan. Pretty snazzy, he thought. He went to the living room windows and opened the curtains to a view of the tree-lined street resplendent with other charming brownstones and a small apartment building on the corner. He smiled at the realization that the attorney, whose life he had taken over, lived pretty much the way he liked to live...only he did it without having to look over his shoulder constantly.

Michael undressed, took a shower and checked out the

closet for clothes. Finding nothing casual, he checked out the huge armoire and found Levis and tee shirts. He chose a pair of jeans and a black tee shirt and then stepped in front of the full length mirror in the corner. It was the first time he'd had the courage to look into a mirror since he'd returned and found himself lying on the floor of O'Hare. He gasped in surprise.

The image he saw looking back at him was so close to the image of Joe that they really could have been brothers. This guy was a bit over six feet and lean. He wasn't as muscular as Joe had been, but he would begin taking better care of his body. Dark, curly hair cut short, framed a square face and intense blue eyes with dark lashes stared back. Michael let his breath out in a whoosh. In his surprise, he didn't even realize that he'd been holding it.

"Thanks, Moses," he said softly, "and...I'll do my best."

He went out to the kitchen and checked out the refrigerator and the cupboards. Boy, Moses wasn't kidding when he said this guy didn't eat right, he thought. The only thing he found in the refrigerator was some dried-up processed cheese spread and a package of crackers along with a can of ginger ale. The cupboard contained a single jar of peanut butter and a bottle of Jim Beam. A loaf of moldy bread adorned the counter. Michael looked around and found the garbage container where he disposed of the cheese, the crackers and the bread. Food shopping was definitely at the head of his "to do" list.

Going back into the bedroom, he pulled a black sport jacket from the closet, grabbed his keys and went outside. The evenings were already beginning to cool down, he noted. He paused on the stoop, squinting against pink glow of the setting sun. Michael took a deep breath of the warm air and smiled. He decided to go for a walk…a simple walk in the park. It would do his soul good, he thought. After his walk, he'd find a Whole Foods Market, and do some much-needed organic grocery shopping!

May 12…

Michael was led into the library of Michelangelo Costanza's home and asked to wait. He was offered a drink, but politely refused. The butler bowed and let himself out quietly through the solid oak double doors. Michael patted the pocket of his suit jacket knowing he would feel the bulk of an envelope there, but checking to make sure anyway. He had dressed in a black Armani suit for the occasion. Coupled with the white silk shirt and the dark grey silk tie, he was dressed for power.

Michael looked around him. The room was probably fifty by forty feet with wide plank oak flooring which glowed with a soft patina. A massive stone fireplace occupied a third of one wall and shelves in varying heights filled with books, art and statuettes occupied the rest of the walls that rose two stories high. Three huge skylights graced the angled ceiling. A simple desk with a glass top resided at an angle in one corner and an ergonomically correct chair sat behind it. A few comfortable wing chairs and a sofa sat casually around the fireplace with reading lamps and small tables close by. Double French doors led out onto an enormous stone patio upon which comfortable outdoor furniture and umbrellas were placed to shield visitors from the relentless sun.

Michael wisely assumed that visitors who were not family members were most likely ushered into this room of the house first simply for the impression of scholarly wisdom and opulence that it conveyed. Michael was not impressed. He thought he could detect the faintest odor of brimstone in the air.

Michelangelo Costanza swept into the room precisely ten minutes after Michael arrived. He too was dressed for power, but in navy instead of black. The suit elongated his compact frame, but there was only so much you could do with five feet, six inches Michael observed wryly. With him was a tall, rail-thin, confident-looking man of about forty, who was introduced to Michael as Carl Silverman. Michael had never met him, but knew him to be the families' consigliore…their legal counsel. Costanza didn't explain Silverman's presence at the outset but Michael knew that once he had explained, when requesting the meeting with Costanza that he was an attorney, the family had to be represented.

Costanza gestured towards the fireplace seating.

"Please, sit, Mr. Lambrusco and make yourself comfortable while we discuss whatever it is you came here to discuss. May I offer you a drink – alcoholic or otherwise?"

Michael politely refused the drink. He reached into his jacket pocket and extracted the thick envelope that he silently offered to Costanza. Costanza looked at the envelope and smiled vaguely as he reached for it.

"I think that this should speak for itself," Michael said.

Costanza opened the envelope and glanced briefly at the document. His thin lips tightened. He began flipping pages rapidly and paused when he saw the signature and the name under it at the end. He looked up at Michael.

"What is this? Some kind of joke? What is this crap?" he demanded, sitting at the edge of his seat and rattling the pages in Michael's direction.

"This 'crap' is a legal and binding document, Mr. Costanza," Michael said mildly. "Show it to your attorney, there. I'm sure he'll be able to verify that fact.

"You see, my brother, Joe…"

"Whaddaya mean, your *brother*," Costanza sneered.

"Joe didn't have a brother!"

"I beg to differ, sir," Michael said. "Our parents would tell you otherwise, were they still alive.

"Joe and I," he began again, "had a, shall we say, difference of opinion, several years back. Since that time, we barely spoke, but we did keep track of one another's whereabouts. Two years ago, he called my law firm and told me of some concerns he had regarding his future. He wanted to have an 'insurance policy' so to speak. He came to Chicago where my firm is based – he came in February – you can check the airline on that, by the way – and I drew up these papers for him. They were witnessed by the senior partners of the firm, although the partners did not know anything about their contents. Attorneys will sometimes witness papers for other attorneys without so much as glancing at them. Professional courtesy, you understand.

"In any case as you can see, my brother recollects names, numbers, dates…all sorts of interesting information. His orders were that these documents were to stay in the vault at the firm unless or until something happened to him."

Carl Silverman had gone over to the desk, turned on the halogen lamp there and was intently reading the pages before him. Costanza glanced at him. "Anything, Carl?" he asked, his tone as cold as ice.

Carl peered up at Costanza over the tops of his wire-rimmed glasses. "Well, yes. Definitely, something," he replied.

Costanza looked at Michael whose face was impassive. He slid from where he had been sitting over to a chair that sat at a right-angle to Michael. He leaned over, and spoke in barely a whisper.

"You know, sonny-boy, I could have you offed right here in this house. I have twenty-three acres of property out there and no one would hear a thing. Could chop you into pieces and use you for mulch. Whattaya think about that?"

Michael stared placidly into Costanza's cold, flat eyes.

"I don't think you'll do it. And do you know why?" Michael continued speaking without waiting for an answer. "I don't think you'll do it because you don't know how many people have a copy of those papers and you don't know who those people are. And even better than all that…if you 'off' me, as you suggest, and these papers become public knowledge – and I have no doubt that they would – your buddies will string you up faster than you can take your next breath, because they're implicated in this too. You got *me*, Micky?"

Michelangelo Costanza jerked at the familiar term of his name. Only the closest members of his famiglia called him Micky. He stared into Michael's eyes for a beat and then looked hastily away.

He turned back. "I got something to ask you, brother of Joe. Where've you been for the past year?"

"A fair question," Michael replied. "I've been living in Paris. I had some business to conduct for my firm. I actually returned about six weeks ago, but I was busy filing papers on the Paris job and didn't have a chance to catch up on everything. It'd been over two years since Joe had been in contact and no one made a connection – and, no one knew Joe was my brother. You see Joe used our mother's maiden name, and not our family name. He'd had it legally changed about nine or ten years back.

"I will confide something else in you, Micky." Michael grinned inwardly as Costanza winced at the offhanded use of his familiar name. "I don't want to toot my own horn, so to speak, but last weekend I had a barbeque…sorry you weren't invited by the way, but amongst those invited were the Chief Justice of the Supreme Court, the District Attorney, the Attorney General, the partners in my law firm, the New York City Police Commissioner, a few distinguished New York City detectives and even a few cops I've made friends with along the way. It's your guess as to who amongst them has those papers in his security box with orders to open them should I meet an untimely demise or suddenly disappear from the face of the Earth."

Costanza glanced up at the man sitting at his desk who

was holding his head in his hand as he read. "Carl," he said in an authoritative but quiet voice. "Where do we stand?"

"Somewhere between prison and hell," Silverman said in a dull voice.

"You know, son…" Costanza began.

"I am not your son. Do not call me that again." Michael immediately admonished.

"Sorry. You know," he began again, "I got where I am because I've got good instincts. I know when I'm being hustled and when someone calls it straight, and I know when to advance and when to retreat. OK. You got me. I'm retreating. Now how far back do I go?"

June 22…

Ava and Michael sat sipping coffee at Starbucks on Main Street in Berkley Heights. They were both on their second cup and they'd been sitting there in quiet conversation for over two hours now. He could understand why Joe had been ready to give up everything for this gentle, fragile soul.

Michael had given Francine Costanza another envelope from his jacket on the day he'd met with Ava's father, and had requested that Francine deliver it to Ava. Michelangelo Costanza had looked suspiciously at the envelope, but had said nothing. Francine had been called into the library when her husband had finally admitted defeat. She had been asked to sit in on the rest of the meeting, the gist of which was that Costanza was to give up all his enterprises over a pre-determined period of time, save for his first enterprise – a small Italian restaurant which he still owned in Brooklyn and even there, all personnel would be given notice. Francine's sister and her husband would take over the running of the business, hiring their own help. Francine had looked at her husband's now weary face and then turned to search the face of their visitor. His eyes softened as he returned her stare and she, in turn, smiled imperceptibly.

Costanza slumped in his chair…a little king defeated…his empire gone. He was to tell all his cohorts that failing health was forcing him to close down operations and his sons were pursuing their own interests with his blessing.

In his letter to Ava, Michael briefly explained his relationship to Joe and begged that Ava meet him because Joe had told him about her, and Michael wanted to tell her some things about Joe. He left his phone number with her and asked that she call. She contacted him a week later. She had so many questions, she said, and only a brother would know all the answers.

Michael didn't know if he had all the answers. His memory of being Joe was all but gone, but it had been replaced by memories of a childhood growing up with a brother instead of as an only child. His parents, *their* parents, he corrected, had been gone for a long time now, but they would have been proud…of *both* their sons.

THE END

TIME OUT

For some, time unravels
It shows many faces
It speeds up, it slows down
Depending on places...

Patrolman Michael Giordano was tired and hot and frankly, pissed off. He'd switched schedules with Joe McGuire whose wife had just had another baby, and had ended up walking a beat on Tompkins Avenue in Bed-Stuy, Brooklyn – a part of town in which he wouldn't be caught dead. Although, if he didn't keep all his senses on "alert" status he might end up amongst the dearly departed!

After eighteen years on the job, and after being passed over several times for promotions, he was patiently biding his time. "Patiently" being the key word here. It was unusual for him to be so...enduring. In fact, it had been his exasperation with the upper echelon in the department that had lost him his promotions. Now, evidently, how high one rose in the ranks was proportionate to knowing the right people and kissing ass. Since he did not care to compete in a "pucker-up" game, he walked a beat with all the young kids. He would be out soon enough, he thought.

In just two more years, he would turn his back on all of this. No, more lieutenants, no more rotating shifts that made you sleep when you should eat or have hunger pangs at four in the morning, no more reports, and, last but not least, no more weird-o's. Civilian life at least meant that he could walk away and ignore the knot-heads. He'd had to deal with them every day for what seemed like forever and Brooklyn seemed to have more than its share. Any given day could find some loony taking a nose dive off the back of a building, while another one could be found chucking glass bottles at passing vehicles off the front of one.

Giordano paused for a moment under a tattered awning with sweat pouring down his round face. He pulled his handkerchief from his back pocket and shook it out. Taking a deep breath of the dank air, he blew out freely through his mouth as he lifted his cap and mopped the top of his balding head. He took in his surroundings – more out of habit than interest. He shook his head in dismay. This place was not much better than his own end of town, he mused. The sidewalks were cracked and heaving from the occasional tree that had outgrown its allotted four-foot-by-four-foot plot of soil; the storefronts looked...sad. The buildings in general were grimy with soot from passing busses and from the oily black stuff that the chimneys of the factories just south of Eastern Parkway belched out all night long.

This once had been a thriving neighborhood where people bustled about shopping, kids played on their stoops and neighbors knew each other. They would watch out for each other and for each other's kids. Folks knew when Mr. Hobson came home from the hospital after breaking his leg falling on the ice, and they brought the old gentleman hot soups and fresh baked goodies. When Sara Ryan's husband passed away, leaving her alone with two small children, the other mothers in her building got together and took turns watching her kids five days a week so that she could keep working at the bank and not have to go on welfare to feed her family. That was the way it was.

Yeah, he thought – was. No one really gave a damn anymore and his job had come down to just watching the neighborhood fall to pieces and seeing the thugs take over, and all the policing in the city never stopped them. For every slime-ball they took off the streets, there were two more to take his place.

So here he was, patrolling an area that would, in his considered opinion, be better off burning to the ground. Another happy day in the life of a New York City cop!

Giordano shook his head in amusement at the jaded tone of his own thoughts. He mopped his face once more and replaced his sodden handkerchief in his back pocket. There were days on patrol when he couldn't decide which was worse – feeling like you were going to pass out from the heat, or being frozen from head to toe by the cold. It was, he admitted to himself, a toss-up.

Giordano hitched his pants up over his capacious abdomen and automatically patted his weapon and nightstick as he began walking once more. The feel of their hard bulk always reassured him.

He dwelled momentarily, upon a time when he'd had high hopes of someday being made a lieutenant, or maybe even chief and being part of the "elite" New York City Police Department. But, that had been a long time ago, when his hair was still thick and dark and his eyes a clear blue and not cynical because of the facts of life he'd learned, both on and off the job. He shook his head slightly in an effort to banish the sullenness that had suddenly befallen him. Morose was not his typical state of mind.

He looked around and sucked in another deep breath. His trained eye took in his surroundings as he visually swept the street he was patrolling. The grime that had discolored the brick and concrete of the buildings had not missed sliding its way in muddy streaks across the glass store fronts, but the interiors still appeared relatively cool compared to the blazing heat of the asphalt beneath his feet.

There was a meat market, whose most ardent customers at the moment seemed to be flies, an abandoned bakery, a small grocery store with dirt-streaked windows, a dry cleaner and an old fashioned mom and pop ice cream shop. Giordano's pace slowed. The logo "Albert's Ice Cream Parlour" was painted in old fashioned Playbill print in a semi-circle on the front window. The print, which was once a shiny gold, outlined in black, had faded to a dull brass, with small scratches of paint missing, but the windows themselves were spotless and gleamed even in the corners. An old style curtain rod was suspended about two feet up from the bottom of the window casing, and a crisp, red checkered curtain hung on it from large wooden rings. The windowsill was equally well kept, and a small menu stood in the left hand corner listing their limited bill of fare.

The obvious neatness of the little store, settled in amongst the surrounding squalor was an anomaly, and the eye-soothing darkness inside beckoned an inviting finger at the over-heated constable. Before he was aware of having made a decision, he found his hand grasping the handle of the green, wooden screen door and tugging it outward.

He got on his radio and called in a code ten/twenty. He was taking a break for lunch.

The coolness of the darkened store caressed his skin and the scent in the air tugged at his memory, reminding him of childhood and trips taken with his aunt and his cousins for ice cream on Sunday afternoons after dinner. It was another lifetime ago, but he could still remember it all so clearly! He and all his cousins would be running around crazy at Nonna's house after dinner, and the grown-ups would be at their wits end with the boisterous children. Then, aunt Katie, the youngest of all the aunts there, would gather up all the kids and take them to Pops Ice Cream Parlor for a dish of their favorite. By the time they got back to Nonna's, the adults had had time to enjoy their espresso and cannoli and the kid's energy level had dropped. A very productive excursion, indeed.

His nostalgia deepened as his eyes adjusted from the blinding sunlight outside to the relative dimness within. He became aware of the booths along both sides in back. They were a dark, heavy wood, polished to a mellow sheen. The red (were they leather?) seats in each, were comfortably cushioned. Triple, black wrought iron hooks were placed high between the backs of each seat, meant for the times patrons had a coat or sweater to hang. The floor was fashioned from small, hexagonal, black and white tiles, and white overhead schoolhouse globes illuminated the innermost recesses. Two large, four-blade fans rotated lazily between the lights. An old Rockola jukebox sat kitty-corner in the rear, inviting anyone with a nickel to come play a tune.

Giordano realized he was gaping and snapped his mouth shut. He turned as he caught a movement from his left, and for the first time, noticed the figure behind the black marble counter.

He took a seat atop a red (leather again?) stool, and smiled absently as the old gentleman handed him a spotless menu. Giordano took off his sunglasses and glanced around behind the counter. He took note of the gleaming chrome fountain spigots with their white enamel knobs, the immaculate, deep-freezer against the back wall and the shining, transparent soda water bottles lined up trimly on glass shelves in front of the sparkling mirror which ran the length of the counter.

"I said, is there something I might get for you, officer?"

Giordano grunted, startled out of his reverie. He must have really been day-dreaming, he thought. He'd never even seen the old man set up his table ware – and with a cloth napkin that matched the curtain in the window, he noted, not without some surprise. A large, glass tumbler filled with ice cubes and water tinkled beside his knife. He suddenly realized he was parched.

He held up one finger, indicating he needed a moment and took a deep, long draught of the deliciously cold liquid before answering.

"Wow! I really needed that. I'll have a burger, medium rare, and fries and a chocolate egg cream, Pops. Thanks."

The old man smiled and nodded obligingly and went through the swinging doors that led to the little kitchen out back, where the cooking was done.

The cop grinned unwittingly as he watched the old man shuffle out back to make his lunch.

He sure matches this place, Giordano thought, noting his crisp, white shirt rolled neatly to the elbows, and his red satin vest and black bow tie. An immaculate white apron was tied securely about four inches above his waist, protecting his shirt and black trousers from stains, though Giordano didn't think a stain stood a chance in here.

His mind wandered again, thinking about the neighborhood in which he'd grown up. It was an OK block, relatively speaking – Ninth Street west of Prospect Park. Saint Thomas Aquinas grammar school, which he'd attended for eight years was a short walk away and, aside from the occasional fight with some kid who didn't know better, life there was pretty decent. Nobody had much money then, but most everyone ate three meals a day and had clean clothes, and that, his mother was fond of reminding him, was all anyone could ask for.

His old block had steadily taken a toboggan slide downhill – destination: slum. He felt sorry for the few old-timers who were still left, trying valiantly to keep their old brownstones from going to rot, but it was a losing battle. What the mice and rats weren't munching on, the roaches were crawling over.

For the second time that afternoon, Giordano was startled out of his pensive mood by the proprietor.

This time, it was the chink of the heavy, white oval plate against the black marble countertop that returned him from his reverie, as the old man placed his meal before him.

His food was hot and fragrant, with fried onions peeking out from under the perfectly toasted burger bun, and a huge sour pickle adorning the side of his plate. Another plate held his hot, thickly-cut fries.

"Ketchup, officer?"

"Yeah, please, thanks."

A meal that looked this good deserved his undivided attention Giordano fervently hoped that his radio wouldn't rattle into life before he'd finished eating, the way it usually did.

He took a tentative sip of his chocolate egg cream and was not disappointed. Just right. A perfect balance of chocolate, milk and seltzer. Too much milk made it bland. Too much seltzer made it shoot unpleasantly up your nose. But this...this was perfection.

Michael savored his meal. The foul mood which had accompanied him on his beat ebbed, and was replaced by a feeling of well-being and simple gratitude for the small pleasure of the meal he'd been afforded.

The screen door to his left flew open and a burst of children sprinted exuberantly through, chattering like so many magpies. The young woman accompanying them laughed and waved hello to the proprietor and trailed behind as they headed for the booths in back and clamored in, switching places with each other several times before finally settling in.

The old man ambled to the back and chatted briefly with the woman and her dark curls bounced up and down as she spoke. She laughed lightly at something the proprietor said and, even from a distance, Giordano could sense the level of comfort between them. Orders were then taken, amidst much giggling and silly prattle and within a few minutes, the old man was back behind the counter, setting up various dishes and soda glasses.

Suddenly, the old jukebox sprang to life and an old Elvis tune, whose name Giordano could not remember, reverberated throughout, much to the delight of the young patrons. Several of the children tumbled into the aisle and waved their arms and gyrated happily in time to the music.

A warm glow invaded Giordano's somewhat jaded spirit. After so long on his job, and after dealing with snot nosed, wise ass brats, it was really nice to see kids who were just plain kids – laughing and dancing and having fun.

He found himself returning the smile of a small boy who sat in a booth facing his way. The boy was young – perhaps seven or eight years old, with dark-brown curly hair, tousled from play and damp from the sweaty heat outside. He grinned self-consciously as the policeman continued smiling at him.

Something about that grin struck a familiar chord in Giordano.

Just like a thousand other seven-year-olds Giordano thought...

But not really just like.

He polished off the last of his burger and looked around for the familiar "No Smoking" symbol. Not spotting one, he relaxed and lit up his Camel, letting his stool swivel around as he relaxed.

The kids were busily slurping, licking, spooning and savoring their various forms of ice cream, and the noise level had dropped considerably. The children's young supervisor was busily spooning some strawberry ice cream into a small, open mouth, and Giordano's gaze meandered over to the little boy again, who was busy with his chocolate ice cream soda – Michael's own favorite when he was a child.

Something was so hauntingly familiar about the child that Giordano found himself staring. The child looked up and met the policeman's stare openly.

Giordano's gaze wavered and he swung his stool back toward the counter.

"'Scuse me. Can I have my check, please?" he asked.

The proprietor smiled and brought out his small order pad, quickly calculating the bill. He tore it off the pad and placed it in front of Giordano, face down.

Giordano had already pulled out his wallet and withdrawn a ten-dollar bill.

He flipped the check over for a cursory exam, and his eyes widened.

"'Scuse me, mister. I think you made a mistake here."

The old man came forward frowning, and withdrew the check from Giordano's outstretched hand. He glanced sharply at the bill.

"No, officer. There's no error here. See?"

He rapidly added up the figures in confirmation.

"No, no – I mean look here: Seventy-five cents for a burger, forty cents for fries and a quarter for an egg cream. Christ! How can you stay in business with these prices?"

The old man smiled gently and repeated his statement.

"No, officer. There's been no error here."

Giordano shook his head unbelievingly and handed his check and the ten-dollar bill to him.

He picked up his change which the old man had placed before him, leaving the sixty cents in coin on the counter for a tip. Then, thinking better of it, he dropped down a dollar bill alongside the coins.

First time I ever tipped more than the total bill, he thought.

He slid off the stool, adjusted his cap on his head and nodded curtly to the proprietor.

The old man smiled warmly in return.

"Thank you Officer Giordano. Stop in again sometime, won't you?"

Giordano let himself out, holding the handle of the screen door to push it closed.

("Donta slama the screena door, Mikey – you banga it offa the 'inges,")

Michael heard his Nonna's admonishment, in her broken English, come to him through the years.

"Aw, Nonna..." the small boy's voice would answer.

"Yep. About a hundred years ago, that was!" he said aloud, to no one in particular.

Giordano glanced about quickly, making sure no one had heard him muttering to himself.

The heat outside hit him like the open door of a blast furnace. He squinted against the wavering rays of the sun as he walked to the end of the block and reached into his shirt pocket for his Ray-Bans.

He swore mildly under his breath as he mentally flashed upon his sunglasses sitting on the stool next to the one he had occupied at the ice cream parlor, and he made a quick u-turn.

Giordano walked back almost two blocks and realized he must have passed right by the shop. He turned back once more.

He walked a bit more slowly this time, taking note of each store as he passed by. The laundromat, a meat market, an old closed-down bakery, the grocery store, the dry cleaner and...

his steps slowed...

It was a small store whose cracked plate glass window was streaked with dirt...small patches of brass (or perhaps old gold) paint in a kind of semi-circle could still be deciphered on the glass. The tattered remnants of a red checkered curtain trailed on a rod which was hanging askew in the window. Giordano looked around him on the street and then, slowly, back to the window. There was no screen door – not even glass in the door beyond. Dirty plywood had taken its place.

Giordano stood for a full minute just staring and then slowly approached the old building.

He felt his sense of time and space begin to skate away and balled his hands into tight fists. He made his way to the glass window of the store with faltering steps.

Cupping his hands around his eyes, he peered into the window.

The marble counter top was gone. The stools – most of them anyway – had been ripped from their foundation. The space which the old Rockola jukebox had occupied stood empty. The booths had been slashed and overturned. The overhead globes were smashed and concrete showed thru where tiles were missing on the floor. All the mirrors had been shattered and dirt and cobwebs had flourished abundantly throughout. Shards of glass from mirrors, beer bottles, soda bottles and cigarette butts littered the interior.

His eyes flew from surface to surface, attempting to take it all in. His mind tried to refute what his eyes saw. It was almost a battle to the end.

Finally, he turned away. Despite the heat and the sun glaring down mercilessly over him, he was shivering. His balance had been thrown. His perception, destroyed. His legs felt rubbery, but he fought for control and began to walk away.

Slowly though.

Very slowly.

And, without looking back.

As the sun continued its westward journey, it reflected off the store's window and something inside sparkled briefly.

One stool remained slightly askew on its stand.

It was rusted and sad. The red leather had been worn thin and age had turned the once bright red to the color of an old bloodstain.

A pair of sunglasses lay atop the stool.

Bright and shiny Ray-Bans.

Abandoned in a place that time seemed to have forgotten or perhaps, only just remembered.

THE END

CLAIRE

Almost everyone knew Claire Eberhardt. Her short, shiny, white hair and her startling turquoise eyes that seemed to rivet into your soul were featured on national magazine covers nearly every month. A former marathon runner, she was the fifty-one-year old leader of a prodigious empire.

In general, her followers loved to cook and bake, erect sheds, scrapbook, make their children's Halloween costumes, construct cabinets so their belongings would always be in place and/or at hand, and decorate their homes. They had power tools that were always immaculate, jars with various screws, nuts and bolts attached above their workspace and beautiful English gardens with delicately worn picket fences. These gardens were tended to by all family members. Should, God forbid, any of their flowers become infected by some wandering disease or insect, Claire had the perfect natural solution to handle the situation.

And then there were the "Holidays." Holidays of each season were addressed and re-defining and decorating your living space and baking were the words of the day. Christmas, however was Claire's specialty.   There were trees to be harvested, complete with roots because "disturbing the harmony of nature is *unthinkable*." Decorations, gifts and wrapping paper needed to be hand-made to give the holidays the old-fashioned sense of home and family, and everything was: "marvelous."

In warm weather, you needed to have a "marvelous" dinner party in your huge backyard (preferably next to a lake or a gentle river, and definitely under the shade of a spreading oak tree) for friends and perhaps family to display your "marvelous" technique for cooking lobster and fresh picked corn on your super-size hand-built brick grill. Your garden there would be dotted with all variety of "marvelous" color from the seeds and young plants sown by your loving hands the previous spring.

Claire appeared on carefully selected late night and daytime shows, and her soft voice seemed to make preparing even complicated dishes easy. Building even the most intricate of shelving units became a breeze.

It was all so easy!

She actually had her own thirty-minute long, nationally syndicated show which aired in the mornings from Monday through Friday. Unbeknownst to anyone except her producer, she usually would spend one day a week doing all the shows for the week. Clips of Claire from that one filming were inserted into each show throughout the week.

Her primary staff consisted of fifty men and women who were the best at what they did. Bakers, chefs, craft specialists, landscapers, gardeners, pottery artisans, furniture restorers, architects, florists, painters, photographers – all were represented. Although it appeared that she herself was capable of doing anything and everything – really, she wasn't. She had, at the beginning of her career dabbled in each, but her empire had grown so vast, it became impossible to keep up. Now, there were "idea people." She had full control and would approve of each project at its inception and then would relinquish the actual doing into the hands of the capable agents she had hired.

It made life easier – for Claire. Those agents she had hired – not so much.

She definitely had a full life…full of work and the occasional husband. She'd been married four times altogether, but of the four there was only one she actually gave credence to, and that was her first marriage to Fred – a man with whom she was totally in love. Claire was nineteen when she'd married him and barely twenty when she'd given birth to Sara. They'd lived in her parent's oceanfront home in the Hamptons and her life was a paragon of existence. Fred was ten years older than she. An advertising exec for The Landau Agency in New York City, he spent his weekdays in an apartment in the city and his weekends with his wife and daughter, sometimes surprising them both with a four-day weekend or time off mid-week so that he could spend more time at home. He was as sublimely happy with his life as Claire was with her own.

Claire was beginning to make a name for herself as a potter and was selling her wares to small, carefully chosen gift shops in Hampton Village. Fred was proud of his wife and supported her vision of becoming a recognized local artist.

Sara was approaching her sixth birthday when Claire went to check out a local shop that was for rent. Claire felt it would make a good studio, especially if she was seen in one of the large windows in front, throwing pottery. The wheel would just fit on a platform with a chair and she could get a local plumber to supply running water in a big, old-fashioned sink she would install discreetly in a curved corner there. The other window could exhibit some finished pieces in an antique mahogany china cabinet and serving board she'd purchased at an estate sale. With the doors and drawers opened, she'd have plenty of display space. It would be…marvelous. She even had a name picked out – Marvelous Makings.

Two weeks after she'd approved the space, Claire was signing the papers for the lease. A florist had wanted to rent the space, but Claire offered the owner of the shop a small stipend to be allotted in twelve monthly payments with a balloon payment at the end of the lease – off the books, of course. The owner smelled money then – excessive amounts of money. He offered a lease with an "option to purchase" clause at the end of the lease period which was five years. Claire signed the lease and purchased a magnum of Moet & Chandon Dom Perignon Luminous. She and Fred would celebrate tonight after Sara was sleeping. She anticipated an evening of sipping champagne and sweet lovemaking.

What Claire did not anticipate was George Adams, a golfer who'd celebrated his par seventy-five at the Sycamore Golf Course by availing himself of the Club's bar and ordering several rounds for both himself and the entire bar. (He was no slouch, you see.)

He was totally fine to drive he assured his golf buddies. Yes, yes, totally fine.

It was seven-thirty p.m. on Wednesday, the seventeenth of July. The intoxicated George cruised along in his Maserati Levante at over eighty-five miles per hour on the Sag Harbor Turnpike and he was totally fine. And he would have continued to be totally fine but for the fact that Route Twenty-Seven intersected with the Sag Harbor Turnpike at one point. Fred was driving west on Route Twenty-Seven. He was a very responsible driver and carrying precious cargo in his back seat. He stopped at the intersection, carefully checking both ways.

Fred began crossing, turned and froze when he heard the screech of brakes and, in slow-motion, saw the passenger door of his Lexus is350 begin to crumple. It struck him at that point, that he probably wouldn't have to seek out a more gas efficient model next year. He turned to look at his daughter for the last time, an apology dying on his lips.

The two Suffolk county policemen who came to Claire's massive front door looked embarrassed and uncomfortable. Accompanying them was the precinct's psychologist who was there to offer whatever moral support that could be offered. Given the gravity of the situation, she didn't suppose much could be done.

Claire expected the police standing and shuffling their feet in her grand front hall were there to request a donation. After all, she was a regular contributor to the Police Athletic League. The fact that they were there to tell her the worst news she could possibly expect to hear never entered her mind.

"We…have some rather disturbing news." Sargent Clayton began.

"Does your husband drive a Lexus is350?" Lieutenant Morrison questioned.

Claire frowned. Fred had probably gotten tickets for speeding, neglected to pay them and had gotten the car impounded. Sara was with him too. Probably wanted Claire to pick them up.

"Yes. Yes, he does. What did he do now?" Claire questioned with a laugh. "Forget to pay a ticket?"

"Well, it's a bit more serious than that."

When they told her that both her husband and her daughter had been killed, she shook her head in denial. No. They could not be dead. That was impossible. No. This could not happen. Her life was…unique. She had basked in the sunshine of birthright. She had made the right choices – albeit rather early in life, of husband and then of child. Her child…her beautiful Sara…she wasn't…dead. Dead was old people…Dead was her grandfather who'd died at ninety-two. Dead was her grandmother…who'd died five years later at ninety-seven. *Her* perfect life was still ahead of her. Her Fred…and worse, their Sara…it wasn't true. These people…these people telling her that her life was irrevocably changed   in   a   matter   of   moments…they were…crazy…weren't they?

# # #

Claire spent the next twenty-two months in an exclusive sanitarium known simply as The Shores. It had been deemed "necessary" by her physician and two psychiatrists. Essentially...she had been committed.

This was a place only the very privileged could afford. She had her own private suite at The Shores. It was akin to her own bedroom at home.

She looked around on her first morning there and shook her head. "No. Those must be covered."

Claire pointed to the mirror over the fireplace. "If there are any more, I want them covered too."

The director of The Shores looked up in surprise at his newest resident.

"Oh, I'm so sorry," he offered. "We didn't know it was against your religion..."

"It has nothing to do with my religion," she fairly shouted. Then she took a deep breath, attempting to calm herself. "It has nothing to do with my religion. I just want all the mirrors covered...please."

The director obliged.

The Shores was a place of escape. There were spas and pools and hot tubs and a discreetly concealed lock-down wing. Badminton courts and tennis courts were available to all as were the many psychiatrists and psychologists on staff.

She'd been diagnosed by them with affective dysregulation combined with agitated depression – conditions that were non-existent prior to the loss of her family she'd insisted. However, one psychologist was particularly persistent regarding her diagnosis and insisted on Claire taking Prozac stating that even while she was on this mood elevator, she continued to be moody, apprehensive, despairing and restless. However, she began to experience other side effects as well: dry mouth, vomiting, headache, extreme agitation, insomnia. She could not possibly go back to her former life in this condition. She wanted to remove Prozac from her regimen. He disagreed.

Her conflict with Doctor Bloch escalated with each of her visits.

"You're wrong!" Claire shouted at one particularly maddening session. "I am not depressed. I just am not a 'depressive personality' and I certainly don't hate myself."

"Then why," he asked, "did you cover your mirrors?"

"You know what? I want another doctor." Claire retorted.

"I suppose you would like someone who agrees with you more?"

"No, you twit. I want someone with half a brain. Someone who can diagnose me properly so that I can get the hell out of here. I need to return to my normal life and I don't need to go there puking my guts out or with these damned migraines. This is worse than I was before."

Doctor Bloch sat straighter in his chair. "Your 'normal' life no longer exists. Your husband and your child exist no longer. You must make peace with that fact if you are ever to move on."

Claire was fed-up and she was not about to take any more. She reached for her water bottle which sat upon Doctor Bloch's desk and in doing so, knocked it over, spilling the water.

"How clumsy of me," she murmured. "My apologies."

"No need." At that, he turned and rummaged through his bottom desk drawer. "I have some paper towels in here somewhere."

"Let me help," she said as she rose from her chair in front of his desk, and made her way around it.

"I'm a very wealthy woman, you know. We could do this little dance all day – me telling you I'm not depressed and you basically telling me to 'get over it' or…"

Looking up for the first time, Doctor Bloch sensed something amiss. "Or…what?" He asked frowning.

Claire smiled. "Or, this…" She opened her mouth and began to scream, tearing at her blouse and running her fingers through her hair like a woman possessed.

As a now very concerned Doctor Bloch began to rise, Claire grabbed the front of his shirt and yanked him off his feet. And, that was how his secretary found him – atop Claire who was sprawled on the floor and ostensibly pushing at him, her skirt hiked-up and tears rolling down her face.

"He…he was holding my mouth," she explained. "I couldn't scream. I couldn't do any…any…" She broke down sobbing.

Doctor Bloch was adamant about his innocence, but was quietly dismissed and seeking employment by the end of the next week. The director determined that a woman who could afford a suite at The Shores, plus a sizeable donation to the newest wing they were adding; well, she just could not be offended, could she?

Aside from all the physical activities at The Shores, there were chess tables. These interested Claire the most. The strategy involved fascinated her. The evaluation of chess positions and setting of goals and long-term plans for the future were something she could relate to. Originally, she'd considered The Shores a place to escape the reality of her own misery and now, she had a plan …a plan for her future.

She was given prescriptions for mood stabilizers (no Prozac) upon her release, and an appointment to see Doctor Anthony Egan in one week. Claire promptly tore up the prescriptions and cancelled the appointment. She did not need anyone or anything now that she'd made her decision. Her family was gone. She would forge ahead and God help those who even attempted to stand in her way.

Claire was a woman driven by grief and her conglomerate empire had its beginning.

# # #

Mike Palmer, his wife, Jenny and their brood of three – Joshua who was fourteen – and would be fifteen in two weeks (he was beginning a countdown), Molly who was eleven and Abigail who was ten, sat huddled together at the top of Cadillac Mountain. It was three o'clock in the morning on Tuesday, the sixteenth of August. Abby kept complaining about the cold, Molly had fallen asleep under her blanket and Joshua kept asking why he had to get up at two-thirty a.m. to "look at some stupid stars." Mike just looked at Jenny and smiled.

"Told you." he simply said.

"I don't care," Jenny replied. "This is a once in a lifetime thing. We're certainly not coming back here anytime soon and they certainly won't be this age if and when we do. So the probability of all of us being all together here ever again is…well, non-existent."

Mike just looked at Jenny and grinned at his tall, willowy wife. He pulled her closer to him, more from the cold than to express his feelings. She shivered.

"You know you're nuts, don't you?"

"Oh, come on Mike," she said, turning inwards towards him. "You know, the best times I remember having with my mother and my sister were the times we spent doing things together. My mom never had a lot of money, but she always made sure she had gas in the car and we would take these weekend trips – to pick pumpkins or apples in the fall or peaches in the summer. We would go to the park and climb hills and look at the stars or paddle a boat in a lake. When we were on summer break, we would go to the beach or to Mom's friend's house at the lake and spend some of our summer vacation there. It was never about money – just time we spent together.

"My point here is, these are the times the kids will remember with us...even though they are whining and moaning about it now. It's what my sister and I used to do!" she said brightly.

"I wouldn't know," Mike said. "Remember? I was an only child."

Jenny looked full-on at Mike. She'd always been drawn to the hulking football player types when she was younger, but instead had married an attractive, tall, slim, nerdy-type. Attractive, but nerdy nonetheless.

"Boring." Jenny stated flatly, still smiling at the thought.

"Tell me about it." Mike replied.

On the way back to their room at the motel, the kids slept in the back seat of their Ford cross-over with the heat running full-blast. Mike drove – tired, but contented. His bonus had covered the price of this vacation in Maine and was proving to be well worth it. They'd decided to visit Acadia National Park in part because it was only eleven hours driving distance from their Long Island home. It definitely boasted enough attractions to keep them all busy for their ten vacation days. There were beaches, hiking trails, carriage and trolley rides, kayaking, rock climbing, moose and black bears to search for. Literally dozens of lobster houses kept them all satisfied. Well, *almost* all of them. Of course, Josh wouldn't eat a lobster if his life depended upon it. Mike had given Josh a cold, hard look when he'd said that lobsters were just giant cockroaches who lived underwater.

Of course, Mike had had to bite down on his own cheek to keep the loud guffaw from escaping his lips. Kid had a point!

Josh's food of choice was cheeseburgers and had been for most of the fourteen years of his life. If by chance the world ran out of cheese or the burgers upon which to put them, he would, most likely, starve. Josh was not adventurous at all where food was concerned. Their first-born child was very single minded. Mike claimed to have the same outlook when he was Josh's age. He comforted Jenny by telling her that Josh would outgrow it. After all, he had!

Molly, however, was a typical middle child. She was lithe, blond, blue eyed and an eleven-year-old replica of her mother. Always trying to please everyone and usually failing on one end or the other, she remained in one of two states: blissfully happy and unaware or whiny and angry at everyone in general. On this trip, she seemed to be leaning mostly towards her blissfully happy side much to the delight of her parents. She'd had her moments, but they seemed to be few and far between.

Then there was Abigail. Abby was tall and willowy and would grow to be a stunning woman with her dark green eyes and thick dark-brown, almost black hair. At the age of ten, Abby delighted in teasing her brother, irritating her sister, mostly ignoring her father and playing up to her mother who was either oblivious of this, pretended to be or perhaps sort of liked the unswerving attention from her last-born.

They were your average American family of five.

Their seventh day in Acadia found them in Jordan Pond House restaurant having lunch outdoors which Jenny had always found an ordeal. People passing by their table in close proximity, bugs buzzing around the food and heat were constant enemies.

Much to her delight, however, all the tables were set well apart on the grass, bugs seemed to be pretty much non-existent and the weather had been quite cool and comfortable throughout their trip. Umbrellas were set up at each table so that even the blazing sunlight became a non-problem.

Unfortunately, the blazing sun had suddenly found all these deep grey and purple clouds to hide behind and then it started to drizzle and moments later, downpour – the kind that had you wringing out your hair at the end of fifteen minutes, so that now the idea of strolling around Bubble Pond after lunch was quite unappealing to all.

"It's OK guys," Mike said to the kids as they dove, en masse, into the shelter of the restaurant. "At least we got to finish our lunch before the rain started and we can come back another day to check out the Pond. Maybe we'll do it on Friday before we leave. We can come down early in the morning, have breakfast, check out the Pond and then head home. We're not in any rush you know."

Only Josh protested. "I'm supposed to meet Willie and Patrick and go bike riding Friday afternoon. I told them I'd be home Friday."

Jenny took a deep breath. "Well, Josh, unless we took a rocket, even if we left right after breakfast at eight or nine o'clock, there's no way we'd get home before nine o'clock on Friday night. We *are* five people – remember? Someone is always complaining that they need a bathroom break, we need to fill the car with gas when we stop somewhere *and...and"* she held up a finger and continued when Josh began to protest, "We do have to stop to eat. Neither Dad nor I can drive for hours without stopping to have a bite and it's safer to take a break every few hours."

Josh grudgingly agreed. Stopping for a burger here and there was something he could relate to.

# # #

The rest of their trip had been filled with activities and the only incident had been when Molly had slipped off a rock and had tumbled down a small hill looking for all intents and purposes, like a hedgehog. Her brother and sister had sat down where they stood for fear of falling over. They were laughing so hard, they were losing their balance.

After sending both Josh and Abby withering looks, Jenny fished in her backpack and meted out antibiotic crème and two large Band-Aids. This and her mother's comforting were the only first-aid Molly required. Her brother and sister were appropriately consoling, stifling their giggles under their father's glare.

Friday morning dawned clear and bright. Jenny approached Mike with the idea of going to Bubble Pond first to avoid any crowds and then they could have breakfast at Jordan Pond House and head for home.

"Sounds like a plan to me," Mike said.

They had crammed most of their bags into the car the night before, carefully packing away the few gifts they had purchased. When morning arrived, everyone showered and dressed and, after Mike double-checked to assure himself that nothing was left behind, they were on their way.

Bubble Pond was located within sight of Jordan Pond House restaurant and after checking out the Pond and the bubble rocks, Mike and Jenny thought that having coffee – juice for the kids – and popovers for all were a great idea. They presented their idea to their brood.

"We don't want anything too heavy first thing in the morning and I'd like to get in at least four hours of driving before we have to stop for a bathroom break." Mike said.

The kids concurred and decided to go browsing around the grounds while they waited for their fresh popovers to bake.

"Just stay where we can see you." Jenny called, and then turned to Mike as their server came with their coffee cups, a pitcher of cream, a bowl of sugar, and a carafe of coffee on a tray.

"So. Do you think it was worth it?" she asked as she poured out coffee for them both.

"What? The craziness, the complaints from the peanut gallery, dragging them out of bed every morning, having *no* privacy for ten days, spending the family fortune…?"

Jenny laughed as she poured cream into her coffee. "All of it, husband.

"Everything."

Mike smiled. "Yup. It was worth every single moment. You realize, between Josh's camera phone, your Nikon, my camera and those little cameras we bought for the girls, we probably have close to five or six hundred photos? I was thinking that…"

He stopped when he realized that Jenny was distracted and looking to his left.

"Something I said?" he inquired.

"No…Mike…Isn't that Claire Eberhardt?"

Mike turned to look in the direction of her gaze.

"Claire who?" Mike asked.

"Claire! Claire Eberhardt!" Jenny said a touch of exasperation in her voice.

Jenny noted the look of puzzlement on Mike's face.

"For Heaven's sake, Mike. You know…the recipes, the clothing, the hotel, there are even the cutest pink tools…oh, forget it Mike. She's has a TV show and she has her stuff in a few craft stores and there's a website. She wrote a book too!"

"And she does this all by herself, eh?" Mike inquired innocently.

"Oh, yeah, I'm sure she has helpers and such." Jenny said, missing Mike's jab and taking a small sip of her coffee.

"Little elves, I expect?"

Again, Jenny missed Mike's teasing tone.

"Her target audience is like us – mostly young families…and she's amazing! She does all these things and I have a few of her pieces…garden furniture and such. That fountain we have in the garden…that's hers. Wow! I wonder what…" Jenny hesitated. "Wait a minute. She has a house in…New Hampshire I think, or maybe even around here; I'm not really sure."

Mike just looked at his wife.

"You seem…impressed. I never figured you for a star chaser."

"No, I'm not, but she's…special. I'm going over there."

"Why?" Josh questioned. He'd returned from playing with his siblings and had plopped down next to his mother, listening to the conversation.

"Because I want to say 'hello' and tell her I'm a fan of hers and see if I can get her to sign…something."

Jenny routed around in her handbag, searching for pen and paper. When she found what she wanted, she stood triumphantly. "Be right back!" She turned to leave, but then abruptly turned back towards Mike.

"Well, at least she's accomplished…stuff." she said with a sniff.

He grinned watching Jenny's butt as she made her way across the lawn towards Claire Eberhardt. Mike picked up his own coffee and realized he really did love watching her walk away. Josh too hurried away from their table as Mike looked on. Humph! Really must have been something I said, he thought smiling.

Jenny had wandered over to where Claire's entourage gathered. She unobtrusively (or so she thought) worked her way towards the center where Claire stood, regaling everyone with her story of a local fox. "…and that's when David got out of the car to shoosh him away. I swear, if an animal could look human…" Claire trailed off as she noticed Jenny draw near.

Jenny clutched the map of Maine she held (it was all she could find) and approached Claire. "Hello, Ms. Eberhardt. My name is Jenny…Jenny Palmer, and…"

"Hello. Ms. Palmer, is it? Well, Ms. Palmer," Claire began, her voice dripping with distain. "Did you never learn manners at your mother's knee? And, did she not emphasize that interrupting a conversation is rude? Further, approaching a celebrity or a well-known person when she's obviously on holiday or otherwise engaged is…well, just *isn't* done – at least in *my* etiquette book."

Noting the folded map and the pen in Jenny's hand, she added, "And what is that you have there? A map? How...quaint. You expect me to sign a map? At least you could have had the decency to purchase my book. *That,* I *might* have considered signing." With a feline smile, Claire looked around for approval from her entourage noting with pleasure that they were hanging on her every word.

Jenny felt her face go hot as the group around Claire smirked and some even laughed outright. She turned on her heel to leave and then turned back looking directly at Claire.

"You know," she said, "Speaking of...I would think that that etiquette book you claim to have would have taught *you* better manners!" Jenny held her head high as she walked calmly away.

Calm however, was not her friend at the moment, for when she went back to where Mike and the girls were sitting, she was fairly vibrating from head to toe and she could not determine if it was from being thoroughly mortified in front of those people or from rage. She preferred rage.

"Where's Josh?" she asked.

"Right behind you, mom." he called.

"Oh, OK." she said, distractedly.

Sitting and joining her family, she recounted the events that had passed only moments ago. Mike and her brood were thoroughly shocked. Mike was prepared to go over and give Claire "what-for" but Jenny wouldn't allow it.

"I'm very happy that the man in my life is prepared to defend me, but I don't think I need it now. I kind of had my say, and I've decided to remove my name and my subscription from her website. Humph! That'll teach her! I'm sure she's going to miss my name the next time she checks out her listings!"

Mike just stared at his wife.

Jenny began to laugh. "Well, I feel better than I did a minute ago. Did you all finish eating your popovers? I think I'll take mine to go. How's about we head for home, guys?"

Mike and the kids agreed, but Josh had a thought which he decided to keep to himself momentarily. He definitely didn't like someone putting his mom down and making her feel bad. All she had wanted was a lousy autograph from some dumb woman. That lady didn't have to be so creepy about it.

# # #

When they were back home on Saturday, Jenny had a talk with Josh and the girls. She felt they needed to know that rudeness is not acceptable from anyone – ever. Jenny didn't think that she had gone over the line with Claire, but thought in retrospect, that she could have handled it differently. Exactly how, she wasn't sure.

But Josh felt that he knew. Josh was a staunch advocate of family and friends and knew that kids today had many more platforms available to them to let their opinion be known – thanks to social networking. Josh had followed his mom when she went over to speak with Claire Eberhardt. He'd recorded the entire exchange on his phone's camera thinking that his mom would get a kick out of seeing the video and showing it to her friends. He hadn't expected things to turn out as they did and now, he was really glad he had that video clip.

# # #

Josh could not believe that his video had gone viral. It had been on for less than two days and already it had over one hundred thousand hits.

He'd uploaded the video he'd taken of his mother's altercation with Claire Eberhardt, giving it a little boost at the end by blipping Claire when she had arched one eyebrow and said "approaching a celebrity…just *isn't* done." Josh had gone in for a close-up of her, in his opinion, "ugly" face and repeated it three times at the end of the video. He was rather proud of himself. He'd done a good job of shooting the conflict and decided the best place to air it was You Tube. Most of his friends checked it out regularly and he had his own account. Now the clip was out there for the world to see just what a "biatch" this "marvelous" woman could be.

# # #

"No, Claire. There's not a damned thing we can do about it." Harold Kline said to his client yet again. "The geeks on our payroll traced back the name and address of the kid from the IP address. The video is obviously you having an altercation with a 'fan' and it was put out there by this fourteen-year-old kid who happens to be the son of this woman. If it was a matter of 'he said, she said' we could sue for defamation and probably ruin them, but this is a video. Not much we can do to get around it. It's obviously you and it's obviously his mother and – before you ask – there was no alteration of the video according to the geeks. And, there are *witnesses* to the conflict. Granted, they're mostly all your lackeys, but I can guarantee that not all of them will fold under your threats. Hell, the threat of being jailed for perjury is a lot worse and one of them might even get his fifteen minutes of fame out of it."

Claire paced back and forth in her well-appointed suite that overlooked the Atlantic Ocean. Eyes narrowed, she hissed like an angry cobra. She had the best team of lawyers money could buy and they could not help her out of this miserable situation. The video of her confronting that...that woman was all over the internet and now the media had picked it up. There were news people six deep at her wrought iron front gate and there was no stopping them. She was not even going to be able to leave her own home. Once they smelled blood or the possibility of some being shed, they were like wolves. And it was all covered under the guise of "the public's right to know."

Right to know, my ass. They have no right to know my private business.

Claire's lips tightened as she narrowed her eyes.

"There must be *something* we can do to diffuse this thing Harold. What the hell am I paying you for?" she demanded.

Harold sputtered ineffectively. "Claire, I can only…"

"Only what, Harold? Only stand there with your dick in your hands and take my money?" she snarled.

"Really, Claire. I see no reason…"

"'Really, Claire…'" she mimicked. "*Do* something!"

Suddenly she whipped around. Grunting, she hefted a rather large, rather old vase and threw it into the marble fireplace where it smashed into angry shards of milk glass.

Harold flinched.

"I can only recommend an apology…" he began.

She stopped her pacing and turned abruptly. "That could work," she considered. "Having her apologize publicly…"

"I meant that *you* should apologize – not her…"

Harold T. Kline had thought that Claire was enraged…until he mentioned the circumstances of the apology. He would have sworn that her short hair stood on end and the look of enmity on her face made his stomach shudder in fear.

"I'll get back to you later this afternoon," he said hastily as he backed out of the room. "Uh..later…"

That sniveling bitch, Claire thought, her mind still reeling. Had I known she was recording…had I even *guessed*, I would have had her thrown out of there. I know I can do *something*…anything to make her life miserable. Recording me…*me*! How dare she? Claire picked up her desk set preparing to throw it too against the fireplace, but accidentally knocked over the picture she kept on her desk…her beautiful Sara.

"You know Mommy's right, don't you sweetheart? We have to do something…something to make them understand us."

Claire spoke in a crooning voice to the studio portrait of her daughter. The picture had been taken as a lasting memory of Sara's sixth birthday. And now, that's all it was…a memory. She replaced the picture gently on the desk and sighed deeply, her mind pitching turbulently as if it were a small boat caught at sea in a monstrous storm.

A bizarre thought came to her then and she found herself cackling wildly with the idea. She remembered a line from the original Wizard of Oz when the Wicked Witch of the West rubs her hands together and says (not altogether sanely) "I'll get you, my pretty…"

The fireplace was flanked by two tall mirrors and Claire caught a glance of herself as she turned. She stopped for a moment and slowly stepped closer to the mirror. The eyes of a haunted woman returned her gaze, mouth twisted into a grimace. Who is that, she wondered, her fingertips barely touching her reflection.

She turned and walked away, making tight fists with both hands, not even noticing the blood she drew as her nails dug into her palms.

# # #

Jenny looked around the laundry room, dismayed that two days after arriving home from vacation, she was still doing "vacation laundry." She didn't remember taking this much, but evidence proved otherwise. She'd spent yesterday shopping for all the staples they'd given or thrown away prior to their vacation and in-between, did laundry. And today was going to be a day of more laundry interspersed with school shopping.

The weather had been rainy since they'd arrived back home which had done nothing to alleviate anyone's mood.

The kids all sat around complaining that they had "nothing fun to do." Forget the fact that they had video games, DVD's, tablets, computers, hand-held games and a flat screen TV in each of their rooms. And *books*! Of course, no one would pick up a book unless it was during the school year.

Meanwhile, Jenny was frazzled. She shook her head and grinned.

"Hey all you lazy-bones," she called. "Get dressed and come downstairs. Ask daddy to make you breakfast because we need to do some school shopping today."

She listened for the groans and the protests and sure enough, they came. It was good to know that there were constants in life…death…taxes…and the reluctance of anyone to do anything that vaguely resembled effort unless they directly benefited from such endeavor. Even though they actually *were* benefiting. It was for school but frankly, they didn't care. She bit her lower lip in consternation.

"I don't want to hear it." she called up the stairs. "We need to get new school clothes and shoes and supplies before school starts and remember…it's starting in ten days." She said a hasty, silent prayer of thanks for that. "We need to go shopping before there's nothing left!"

She heard Mike going into the girls' room rousting them from whatever they were doing and then into Josh's room.

He wasn't in there long and called to her as he trotted down the stairs.

"We may have a problem," he said.

"Why? What's wrong?" Jenny asked with a sigh.

"I don't like the way Josh looks, Jenny."

"Big deal. He always looks like that first thing in the morning. You just don't notice because you leave for work before he gets up."

"That's not it, Jenny." Mike said. "He's lethargic and his head feels too hot to me. I think he's coming down with something."

"Oh, great!" Jenny said. "Just in time for school. Well, really we have about ten days, but still. We don't need anything going around. It could be he caught a bug in Maine or he's just jet-lagged."

"Could be," Mike agreed. "But I don't think he needs to be traipsing around a mall for hours either. Let him stay home today. I'm off 'till Thursday and if he feels better by Wednesday, you can take him shopping by himself. If not, you can take him to Dr. Miller and find out what's wrong."

"Hmm…guess you're right," Jenny said. "Maybe you could make the girls breakfast and coffee for me?" she asked hopefully. "We can get to the mall when it opens and if we're lucky, it won't be too crowded. Afterwards, maybe you could take the girls to your mom and let them go swimming in her pool and I can stay here with Josh and finish straightening out the house."

"Sounds like a plan to me." he said planting a kiss lightly on her lips.

"Good. Now, go!" she said grinning.

# # #

While Jenny and Mike were attempting to organize their day, Claire was making plans of her own. She had a strategy and she was putting Step One into action this very afternoon. She signaled her assistant into her office.

"Vittoria, I'm planning a dinner party for Saturday – not this Saturday, but the following. I'd like you to send out formal invitations on this stationery."

Claire was sitting behind her antique, mahogany desk and handed her assistant envelopes and sheets of heavy parchment with her name emblazoned across the top.

"I want the invitations to be hand-printed – calligraphy, of course. And they're to go out to Mr. and Mrs. Sanders, to Dr. and Mrs. Miner and family, to the Ogilvy's and their daughter Melanie, Mrs. Clara Scott and her son, Tyler, Doctor Raymond Borden and to Mr. and Mrs. Palmer and family – not the Corbin Palmers, the Michael Palmers. You can find addresses for all of them in my 'contacts' list and I want the Palmers' invitation hand-delivered. This would be the Palmers first invitation from me and I don't want them to be so surprised they forget to RSVP. Everyone else's can be mailed, by the way. Tell Ryan to wear his uniform, use the Bentley and deliver the invitation to the Palmers personally this afternoon.   He is to wait for a reply and he's to let them know he is waiting."

Claire deliberated for a moment.

"The invitation will be for four o'clock, here, dress is dinner-casual. RSVP by Thursday, next. That's all Vittoria. You may go."

Vittoria mumbled her assent and left, quietly closing the French door behind her. She loosened her grip on the knob of the door and sat behind her desk. Calling up the encrypted file from her computer, she began to work.

And now, we wait, thought Claire as she reclined in her chaise. Let's just see what you make of my invitation and just how guilty you really feel about your internet adventure or should I say, "misadventure." Using the remote, Claire brought up the abhorrent video on the flat-screen and nearly had a seizure when she saw that the video had almost half-a-million hits. She closed her eyes and took several deep, calming breaths. That was all she could do – for now.

Ryan went to deliver the invitation to the Palmers precisely at six p.m. He went to their door, knocked. He tipped his hat and inquired as to the status of the lady of the house when the young girl answered. Molly looked up at the nearly six-and-a-half-foot man, and beginning to lose her balance, tipped precariously backwards. Ryan smiled inwardly, and grasped her hand to steady her.

"Your mom," he said by way of explanation.

He could not believe the very loud and very shrill voice that emanated from this relatively small person.

A somewhat larger version of the child made her way to the front door, a questioning look on her face.

"Yes? May I help you?"

Here at last was someone to whom Ryan could relate.

"Yes, madam. I am to deliver this to either the lady or the gentleman of the house and await a reply."

"Excuse me?" Jenny questioned.

"I shall wait here on the front porch, if that meets with your approval madam."

"I don't understand," Jenny said.

"Perhaps, if you open the envelope?" Ryan suggested gently.

"Yes, yes of course. Would you excuse us? Oh, pardon my manners. Of course, you're welcome to come in…" Jenny said swinging the door wide.

"Thank you madam, but I shall wait…right here, if that…"

"Meets with my approval," Jenny finished. "Yes, waiting there would be fine with me. Just fine."

Jenny backed away, Molly still peeking out from behind her and gently shut the door.

Ryan stood like a statue in the steadily gathering darkness patiently awaiting an answer. Mike noted the Bentley as he peered out from between the closed curtains and asked Jenny why she hadn't asked the chauffeur in to wait.

"He didn't want to come in," Jenny explained. "Said he'd wait on the porch 'if it met with my approval.' I don't know about this, Mike. What do you think? You think she wants to apologize for her behavior last Friday or what? And how does she know where we live?"

Mike looked at his wife disbelievingly. "Hon. We live in the age of the internet. You can find out about anyone…anywhere…anytime. Hell, you could probably find out what someone had for breakfast this morning if you cared to. I mean, it's all out there. And yeah, I guess she wants to make up. Why else the invitation? Maybe she was just having a bad morning or someone had just given her some bad news. I don't know. But someone in her position…" Mike trailed off.

"So, what do you think? Do we go or not go?" Jenny queried.

"It's your thing," Mike replied. "You decide."

Thus, Mike gave Ryan the thumbs-up on the invitation.

And thus, Claire began Step Two of her plan.

# # #

Jenny laughed as Nick Sanders finished his story. She had anticipated feeling very uncomfortable this evening and based on that premise, had accepted the glass of wine that Mike had offered before they left.

"Anything to scare away the whim-whams..." she explained to Mike. "I just don't know what to expect!"

"Don't 'expect' anything either way hon. Just relax and have fun." Mike had suggested.

"You know Mike, I'm not really feeling all that great," Jenny began. "Maybe I should..."

"Listen, Jen. I know she was rude to you and all, but her being rude doesn't justify you being rude in return ...well, not really, anyway. Look, if we go and she's anything less than amiable towards us – ok, towards *you*, we'll leave. Deal?"

"Promise?" Jenny asked, her mouth curving into a smile.

"I do." Mike said, grinning in return.

As it turned out, Mike had been right. Jenny had slipped into her party mode and was having a wonderful time. Their kids were socializing with the other kids there and making new friends and Mike had received an invitation from Sam Ogilvy, a big square of a man, to go fishing on his boat next Saturday. Sam mentioned that he was planning on taking his nephew with him and invited Josh to come along.

"Tyler is thirteen going on forty," Sam admitted. "He lost his dad a year ago, you see. My brother-in-law was a cop who died in the line of duty."

Mike's eyes widened and he saw the shadow pass over Sam's face. "Oh, God, Sam. I'm so sorry to hear that."

"Yeah, well, shit happens. The worst of it was that he was working my shift that day. My wife and I were on an extended weekend and John, that was Tyler's dad, he volunteered to take over for me so we wouldn't have to race back for my shift on Tuesday morning.

"Anyway, I try to take the boy with me as much as I can. My wife and I have a daughter, Mel, but she's only nine so she's no company for Tyler. I take him fishing, camping, hiking and I take him with me when we go downstairs to bowl or swim a few laps."

"Go *downstairs* to bowl?" Mike questioned.

"Oh, yeah," Sam said. "Annie – my wife, is Claire's first cousin so we have an open invitation to come and use the facilities. Claire has a full-sized bowling alley downstairs. There's also a home theatre, a well-stocked wine cellar, billiards tables and the indoor pool – you know, for when it gets too cold to use the outdoor pool."

"Of course," Mike agreed. "Everyone should have an indoor pool for inclement weather conditions."

Sam just grinned.

At that point, Claire made her grand entrance – sweeping down the gently curving center staircase – fully decked out in a black, wide-leg jumpsuit and sparkling, with what Jenny believed to be about twenty carats worth of diamonds. Everyone turned to face their hostess.

"Hello darlings. Sorry to be late to my own party, but I was on a business call to Paris and couldn't cut it short. You know how those French are. They *do* chatter on."

The women's laughter tinkled lightly and the men murmured assent.

Claire stopped and took a moment to speak with everyone as she made her way towards Jenny and Mike.

She reached them a few moments later and after greeting them, said quietly, "I apologize to you on several levels. Firstly, because I was late and couldn't introduce you to everyone, although I see you made it just fine without me."

Jenny watched her skeptically.

Claire laughed easily. "I'm really happy about that, but mostly I invited you here by way of an apology." Here, she paused, looking embarrassed and turned fully towards Jenny. "I cannot excuse my behavior that day in Maine. I can only say that it was one of '*those* days' and I probably never should have left my house. I only hope you can find it in your heart to forgive me."

Jenny was a gentle soul and her heart immediately went out to the woman. She smiled as she said, "I'm sorry it happened, but I do understand." Jenny extended her hand but Claire just smiled and pulled Jenny in for a hug.

"Why shake hands here when we can hug." she said. "You know, I have the feeling that this is the beginning of a beautiful friendship. Would you like a tour of my home? I'd love for you to see my kitchen. Do you bake? I'd really like it if you could come to my 'cookie exchange' after Thanksgiving. I have about five or six friends come in and we have a marvelous time. We each bring our favorite holiday cookie recipe, bake it here…enough for all, of course, and then we exchange cookies. Of course, in between, we're all enjoying wine from my private stock and canapés and good company!

"I have a staff so the best part of it is – there's no clean-up!" Claire giggled conspiratorially. "We girls usually top the day off with a private viewing of a new movie downstairs. What do you think? Does it sound like something you'd like to do?"

Jenny felt overwhelmed but nodded her head. "Sure, Claire. It sounds like…fun."

"Oh that's wonderful, Jenny. I'll keep in contact with you myself but I'll have my assistant, Vittoria, call you with the details. Please leave your cell phone number with Ida – the lovely woman who answered the door tonight. She'll see that Vittoria gets it.

"If you'll excuse me now, I really must circulate."

Claire moved off, leaving a very astonished Jenny behind her.

# # #

Claire was true to her word and called Jenny twice. Once to just say "hi" and once to wish Jenny and her family a great Thanksgiving holiday, and to remind Jenny that the Wednesday following Thanksgiving would be "cookie exchange" day.

"Just bring whatever you need for your recipe," she told Jenny. "Don't worry if you should forget something. I usually have almost anything you need here. I'll still have Vittoria call to remind you of the date and time, of course."

Jenny thanked Claire and promised to see her after Thanksgiving.

# # #

"The cookie exchange was actually fun!" Jenny told Mike the next day. "Claire's friends were really…nice."

"What did you expect?" Mike asked. "Thought they would be bitches?"

"Nooo…" Jenny shrugged, shaking her head slowly. "I don't know *what* I expected."

She turned as she saw Josh enter the kitchen. He grabbed for a doughnut from the box on the counter.

Shaking her head, Jenny closed the dishwasher door, chastising Josh for eating when it was so close to dinnertime. He turned to her, stuffing the entire doughnut into his mouth and grinned.

"Awf, Mumm…" was all he could manage, ducking away from her playful swipe.

"You met most of these ladies when you went to Claire's the first time." Mike said. "Did you think they'd stop speaking with you or turn into weirdoes or what?"

Jenny shook her head without much conviction.

"I don't know Mike. It's just that…these people are out of my league. I mean, if I met them, let's say at a store in the Hamptons even, I just know that they wouldn't speak with me. They'd think I didn't belong and they would probably be right, but I'm telling you, they would have *nothing* to do with me.

"Well, maybe with the exception of Annie Ogilvy. She seemed…*real*. You know? It's hard to believe that she's Claire's cousin." Jenny shook her head with certitude. "The only reason they are sociable is because of their friendship with Claire and I'm not exactly sure of her."

Mike just looked at his wife incredulously.

"Seriously? What do you mean, you're 'not sure of her'? She tracked you down, apologized, called you twice...*twice* here at home – once for no reason other than to talk with you and the other time to wish us all Happy Thanksgiving. Have you ever thought that maybe she was sincere in her apology and maybe, just maybe after talking with you she actually *liked* you? I mean, it's not that much of a stretch. Hell, *I* like you!"

"I should hope so, Mister. You married me, remember?" Jenny laughed as she picked up the spoon from its resting place in order to stir the stew she'd prepared.

Mike went to Jenny and took the mixing spoon out of her hand. He lifted her chin, kissed her firmly and then licked the spoon.

"Needs a bit of salt," he commented. "Wanna take advantage of some of those marriage benefits?" he asked, wiggling his eyebrows lasciviously.

"Sure. Later. I need to finish loading the dishwasher, first."

"Boy, I remember a day..." Mike began rolling his eyes heavenward.

"Yeah," said Jenny, rolling her own eyes for emphasis. "A day when there were no kids and no dishes to clean, and no clothes to wash, blah, blah, blah..."

Mike just laughed.

And, as Mike laughed, Claire was putting the finishing touches on her last and final – Step Three.

# # #

As his mother loaded the dishwasher and Claire made her plans, Josh checked his You Tube video. He supposed he should take it off now that Claire and his mom were sort of friends. It had almost a million and a half hits and Josh was very proud of the piece. He imagined that the reason for its popularity was because a "celebrity" was involved.

Josh had made friends with Tyler Scott when he went fishing with Tyler, Tyler's uncle Sam and his own dad on Sam's boat, and discovered that Tyler felt his aunt's friendship with Claire wasn't genuine. He felt that his aunt and his mom were Claire's "charity work."

"If my dad hadn't gotten killed, I don't think she would've noticed us. We, well, my mom, my dad and me, we lived in the Hamptons for years and she barely said hello to any of us. Then the whole thing about my dad happened and now she's all over us. I can't figure it out."

Josh had not heard Jenny's misgivings about her friendship with Claire, but Josh was a smart kid.

"Yeah, I kinda know what you mean, Tyler. She was a real creep to my mom when we met her in Maine and now she's trying to be my mom's best friend. It just feels phony to me. I'm not sure, but I don't think my mom falls for it either. My dad thinks she's OK though."

Tyler and Josh exchanged phone numbers on the boat that day, and texted each other a few times a week. Josh texted Tyler about the video, wanting his opinion. Tyler told him he had already seen it and had told most of his friends about it. He also said that Josh was becoming something of a celebrity in his own circle of friends in the Hamptons.

'They think it's spot-on' Tyler texted Josh. 'We *all* think she's a phony!'

Josh had an internal debate with himself about the video before the start of school that day and then decided to keep it on You Tube a while longer. Besides, he still got a kick out of watching it. A few – very few – of his friends hadn't seen it when it first aired, but Josh made sure they did. Heck, not one of them had anything on You Tube that had over a million hits, and he was very gratified.

After almost two months of airing the video, it wouldn't make any difference, he thought. If his parents hadn't seen it yet, the probability was, they never would. Most adults don't go on You Tube looking for stuff anyway, Josh reasoned.

He would soon realize his error in that line of thinking.

# # #

Claire had her last step in place and would not have her assistant be the go-between. It was much more like her to have Vittoria make appointments and set things up with people but in this case, the fewer who knew of her plan, the better. And, of course, this was something that had to be done *personally*.

And personal was what it was all about with Jenny, Claire thought. She'll do anything for someone she perceives as a friend and that would be the simpering wimp's undoing.

Jenny received the call not long after Josh received his text from Tyler.

"I'm having a crisis and I need to speak with you." Claire stated flatly when Jenny answered her phone.

"Oh, uh, well…you're welcome to come here. I'll be home all day and the kids won't be back from school until later this afternoon." Jenny said, looking around frantically and attempting to assess the damage around her. She tried to see the house as Claire would see it. She sighed. Claire didn't have kids and hers *did* live here.

"Oh, well, I…" Claire hesitated. "Is there any way you can come here? I would feel a lot more comfortable because, you know, I've always got paparazzi hanging out around me and trying to get candid pix or information. I don't want them following me to your home because then they might start following you – and maybe even your kids."

Jenny thought about this for a moment.

"OK, Claire. Are you sure you want to confide something personal to me? I mean, I'm sure you have friends who are closer to you…" Jenny trailed off.

"No. It's you I need. You know me well enough to be completely honest, and that's what I need." Claire said adamantly.

"OK, then. It'll take me twenty minutes to get decent and about an hour to drive there. I have to be home by five though. Josh can take care of the girls for an hour or so, but I need to make dinner for everyone." Jenny laughed. "I need one of your fifteen minute recipes," she said. "Then I won't have everyone complaining that they're being neglected."

"Consider it done!" Claire retorted with a laugh. "See you."

Jenny disconnected and texted Josh to tell him that she had an errand to run and to ask him to babysit his sisters until she arrived back home.

"I promise I'll be home by five. Five-thirty on the outside." Jenny texted, sure of her return time. "I'll make dinner for all of you when I get home. Tell dad I'll see him later and we're still on for that movie. Love you, and thanks."

# # #

The last thing Jenny consciously remembered was using the door knocker on Claire's front door and hearing the resounding thud from within the house. The gates had been open when Jenny pulled up (funny, but hadn't Claire mentioned paparazzi?) She assumed that they were opened specifically for her, so she continued up the long driveway, parked and walked to the double front doors. The door on the right side was opened a trifle but Jenny used the knocker to be sure. And…now she remembered. She'd opened the door a bit more and poked her head in, calling Claire's name as she did. And she remembered…being stung in the neck…by…a bee?

Now, she found herself lying back in a cushioned chair of some sort. She attempted to lift her hand to her head but found she was unable to move. The first thought that came into her mind was that she'd had a stroke and that thought brought terror into her heart.

She opened her mouth to speak and heard incoherent babble that was, apparently, emanating from her. She began to sob.

"Don't worry, dear. That's the thiopentobarbital sodium – Pentothal to you. You know? Truth serum? Anyway, it's a wonderful barbiturate. You got a shot of it when you walked in the front door! It works very fast and induces a state of complete relaxation. For future reference, it's great for surgical procedures. No lasting effects to be concerned about. It will wear off in a while and then your speech will be back to normal." Claire said brightly.

Jenny tried to pull herself together when she heard the voice. It sounded like Claire, but she wasn't making sense. Jenny looked around and discovered Claire looking down at her. She was sitting comfortably on a stool next to where Jenny lay. She blinked, attempting to clear her vision and focus on Claire's face.

Claire grinned. "Guess I must have given you too much. I think I might have over-estimated your weight, but you'll live – for now."

Jenny looked around her, confusion still licking at the corners of her mind. It was then that she noticed a TV…no, a movie screen in front of her. There was no sound or movement but she saw herself and Claire, surrounded by Claire's friends. As she attempted to process the information, the characters on the screen began to move and gain their voices.

What she watched confused her even more.

She saw the entire confrontation she'd had with Claire on that first day in Maine unfold and re-lived the humiliation she'd felt at Claire's rebuff.

Jenny blinked rapidly and again attempted to speak.

"Whe…How…"

Claire smiled delightedly, amused at Jenny's attempt and rolled her eyes, letting her limbs go slack and putting her tongue between her own teeth, mimicking Jenny's speech.

"That's what you look like, you know. Oh, I forgot to drool. Sorry."

Claire's mouth suddenly twisted into an ugly sneer and she bolted off the stool upon which she'd been sitting so relaxed only a moment before.

"That's what I've had to watch hundreds of times since we came back from Maine. That's what my friends, my family, my customers have seen." Claire's voice was rising until she fairly sputtered with rage.

"That…that…*thing*…that travesty, has been on You Tube since I came back from my well-deserved vacation, thanks to your son. Over a million people have seen it! Do you even realize…do you even *know* a million people? I do. And now, they're all mocking me. *Me*!"

Claire emphasized her displeasure by viciously backhanding Jenny across the face, sending her head rocking.

Jenny's eyes began to water, even as she felt her mind clearing. She was in trouble here…very big trouble. This bitch was crazy and she would have to do some fast and furious thinking to get out of this one – alive.

And Josh. Claire had said Josh had put it on You Tube. That meant Josh was in danger from this lunatic as well.

Jenny had never considered herself an actress – neither was she a liar – but now she'd have to pull off both convincingly to protect her family from this crazy woman.

Jenny closed her eyes against the pain and attempted to think. That slap was done in a fit of temper. However, Claire pretty much seemed to want Jenny aware and alert for the show to come, and she had no doubts that there was a show to come. The only thing that came to Jenny's mind was to persist in slurring her speech, keep her eyes as unfocused as possible and pretend to nod off. Claire might continue to believe that she'd given Jenny an overdose of the drug or that, possibly, Jenny was having an allergic reaction. The only danger was that if she thought she'd overdosed her, she might seek an alternative to wake her up and that could prove to be fatal. Jenny suspected that Claire was not particularly concerned about her fatality because one way or another, that was probably Claire's ultimate goal.

For now, however, it was the only thing that Jenny could think of and the only thing that might get Claire to leave her side and give Jenny time to work out a plan and/or work herself free.

Jenny opened her mouth to speak and looked at Claire in confusion. She garbled out a few incoherent syllables.

The incoherent speech was real, the confusion – not so much.

Claire had been standing over Jenny, shaking with anger. Now, she forcibly relaxed her shoulders and put on an affected smile.

"There now. I feel somewhat better. I've been wanting to do that since that first day in Maine. You just nap now and I'll come back a bit later and we can talk…about you and your family's future.

"Of course, if it were up to me and given a preference…none of you have one!"

At that, Claire turned to leave. She turned back, smiled and said, "I'll just leave the entertainment on so you don't feel lonely.

"Oh, and I hope you don't mind, but I took the liberty of going through your purse and taking your car keys. I put the car into my garage. Pathetic little thing that it is, it wouldn't do to have anyone see it in the driveway."

She gave Jenny a gay little finger-wave, smiled again and closed the doors.

# # #

"What do you mean, 'she's not home yet', Josh?" Mike asked.

"Hey," Josh said. "Don't kill the messenger. All I know is, Mom texted me while I was in school, and told me she was going out. She wanted me to watch the girls and said she'd be home by five or five-thirty to make dinner. That's all I know. See? Look at this."

Josh had been searching through his phone and now turned it so that his father could view the text from Jenny. His father frowned as he read.

"She didn't say where she was going?" he questioned.

"No, Dad." Josh said with exaggerated slowness. "She didn't say anything about where she was headed."

"We were going to the movies tonight," Mike said. "She was going to make a quickie meal – burgers and fries – so we could make a seven-thirty show."

"And what were *we* doing?" Abby questioned.

"Kathy, Mrs. Ryan's daughter, was coming in to watch you guys."

When Mike caught the three just staring at him, he explained, "Number one: It's a school night and Number two: It's a chick-flick."

"So how come you're going?" Josh asked.

"Cause that's what you do when you're married." Mike said. "She didn't say anything to me..." he said scrolling through his own phone. He looked up, frowning again. He wasn't sure of which way to turn. Well, first things first. Picking up the house phone, Mike began dialing each of Jenny's friends asking if they'd seen Jenny and, if not, who else to contact. After exhausting his contact list, Mike returned the phone to its base and considered his next move. Taking a deep breath, he scrolled through his phone, searching for a number. When the line was picked up, he identified himself and began his story.

Mike then called Kathy Ryan and asked if she could watch the kids a while longer than originally anticipated.

"Listen, Kathy. Maybe you could put your mom on alert? Something has happened with Jenny…no, she's fine and I'm sure everything is OK, but I haven't spoken with her all day and I can't locate her. I spoke with an NYPD detective friend of mine and I just want to do some checking around town. Maybe you could ask your mom if it would be OK for you to sleep at our house tonight…at least, until I get home. I mean, you could use the guest room…OK, call me back."

Five minutes later, Kathy's mom was at their door.

"Mike, you do what you need to do," Denise said calmly. "Meanwhile, you can rest easy about the kids. They can sleep at our house."

Mike began to object, not wanting to put her out.

Denise overrode his objections. "Mike, just do what you have to do. It will be a fun night for the kids and I'll order pizza for everyone. They'll be in bed by nine and I'll make sure they get to school in the morning and I'll pack a good lunch for them. Don't worry."

Denise walked the kids over to her house while Mike grabbed pajamas, toothbrushes and clothes for the next day. He snatched up their backpacks as he left, heading next door.

Mike kissed each of his kids. "You don't give Mrs. Ryan a hard time now, and do as she asks."

He looked back. "Thanks, Denise."

Denise waved him off with the backs of her hands and smiled. "Go, go…and good luck Mike. But I'm sure she's just fine. You're probably worried for no reason at all."

# # #

Claire looked in at Jenny three more times and roused her from her specious sleep each time, wanting to begin her "game," but each time Jenny awoke she was as incoherent as she had been originally. After the third time, she vowed to begin her game when she awoke the next morning whether or not Jenny was reactive. Pain was pain, after all and she was sure that her nemesis would be responsive to that particular stimuli although she *had* wanted her to understand the reason behind it.

Claire, in her sweetest voice with no trace of sarcasm, bid Jenny "Goodnight" after her third visit and closed the theatre's heavy door quietly behind her.

Returning upstairs, Claire began preparing dinner for herself. She had given a four-day weekend off to her staff. This was not unprecedented. Approximately four to five times a year Claire would dismiss everyone on a Thursday or even a Wednesday afternoon. It was good for their morale, she reasoned. Of course, this would not interfere with their two to three-week vacation. This was…a bonus.

It was also a bonus for her. This was, of course, not the first "guest" she had entertained in the luxurious downstairs theatre. The builders had soundproofed the room to her specifications. They'd been told she did not want the sound of a movie interrupting the quiet concentration of a wine-tasting nor have a noisy bowling game interfere with a movie.

A turn bolt had been provided for the double doors leading into and out of the theatre.

"I hate interruptions while watching a movie and I don't want anyone in there without my sanction."

It all seemed more than reasonable, if only to her.

In her mind and heart, she felt she should not have to accommodate anyone who gave her grief, directly or indirectly. First it was that character Benjamin Schuyler, the bartender who'd served George Adams. He'd lost his license for six lousy months after it was determined that Adams had a .08 blood alcohol level. Claire had hired him on the pretext that she was having a "party." He was to come to her house for an interview. She knew he'd come. Ben had been fired over the incident and needed money. He'd not been hired by her, but had made marvelous mulch for the garden.

George Adams, of course, had been first on her list. Unfortunately, he'd died three months after the accident from complications, thus depriving her of the pleasure.

Realizing she'd been "lost in thought" yet again, Claire tossed her now cold dinner and put the dishes into the mini-dishwasher. She would not abide an untidy kitchen nor an untidy life and loose ends were loose ends. Originally, Claire had wanted Josh in the same predicament as his mother found herself in, but she'd not counted on Jenny's apparent inability to pull out from under the influence of the Pentathol. Josh was the one who had put the video on You Tube. However, the confrontation with Jenny was the fulcrum upon which the whole circumstance turned. If she hadn't attempted contact with Claire, this situation would never have arisen. Therefore, this was all Jenny's fault!

There had been others who'd slighted her or caused her undue stress and they had been…dealt with…accordingly.

Tidy.

Neat.

Done.

# # #

Jenny, meanwhile, was doing her best to extricate herself from her state of affairs. She had managed to lift her head and get a better view of her circumstances. She found she was sorry she had done so. Claire had brought her into the theatre in the basement of her home and had tied her to one of the reclining chairs. From what Jenny could see by the undulating light of the movie screen, her wrists were tied down to either arm of the chair and her legs tied at the ankles and then to the footrest of the chair.

I am so screwed! OK. Time to buckle down and figure my way out of here.

When Claire had come down to check on her, Jenny had actually been sleeping. She had allowed herself to rest anticipating the need for all of her strength – both of wits and of body to get through her situation.

When Claire came in again, Jenny had been hard at work attempting to release either her hands or her ankles, but had had no success. Since the light of the screen was the only light Claire had allowed her and since Jenny was still rambling, Claire hadn't noticed the abrasions on either her hands or her ankles, and the same held true on Claire's third visit.

Jenny, however, prudently deduced that Claire's fourth visit would not end as well for her. In the darkened theatre, Jenny had lost track of time but assumed it must be late since Claire had said goodnight on her last visit which meant that she had one final chance at freedom. One chance only and she couldn't afford to waste even one moment of that time.

# # #

Mike had gone to see Sam. He knew that the FBI would not consider a person missing for forty-eight hours and he also knew that by then, it would be too late.

Sam encouraged Mike to wait until morning.

"It's way too early to chase her down now," Sam explained. "My Captain would raise holy hell with me. I mean, she's been missing for what now, three, four hours? I can call in a few favors in the morning and get the Electronics Division to do a trace on the phones, but right now…my hands are tied."

Mike knew his wife. They had been together for almost seventeen years – since they were both juniors in college. Jenny was not the kind of woman who just "took off." She was stable; their marriage was better than good and the kids were still too young to give either of them much grief. She had not confided in him about any particular problems she was experiencing, and she always did. They were best friends – which was what made their marriage so terrific.

Things were fine with both her family and his and no, she wasn't having an affair. Why was he so sure? Well, aside from the fact that she would never have had the time, she was always, *always* reachable – which is what worried him now.

She rarely used the land line in the house anymore and relied on her cell phone almost exclusively and now, Mike told Sam, when he attempted calling her, the call was going directly to "voice mail." This could only mean that the phone was turned off, the battery had run out, or she was in a dead zone, which was highly improbable. He highly doubted her battery had run out because she had a car charger specifically to avoid such an issue.

"She never turns off her phone, Sam." Mike said.

Sam merely shook his head when Mike finished his story.

"Well, I don't think you have anything to be concerned about Mike. She might have gone to the mall, met an old girlfriend and they got to talking. She did say she was going out, right? She could have left her cell phone in the car you know – by mistake," he quickly said correctly interpreting Mike's sidelong glance.

Mike agreed, slowly nodding his head. "But, Sam, this is not like her. I mean, even if she did meet a friend, it's what…" Mike consulted his watch, "eight o'clock now? For God's sake, it's dark out Sam. It's been dark for hours now. She's got to know it's later than five or six o'clock."

"OK, Mike. Calm down. We can't do much until morning. Tell you what, I'll pick you up at six a.m. Oh, hey, what about your kids?"

"They're taken care of," Mike told Sam. "They're with my next door neighbor, Denise. She'll get them off to school in the morning."

Mike felt defeated. He agreed to meet Sam in the morning. He knew that Sam would do his best for him and Mike felt lucky having someone to call upon, but waiting around for another ten hours…she could have been in a car accident or she could have been attacked…the possibilities were endless as were the movies playing in his mind of murder and mayhem.

He drove around aimlessly for the next three hours – around the mall, around the small town they lived in and around the back streets of their neighborhood.

The first thing he noticed was the upside-down, burned-out hulk of an SUV. He saw the ambulance as he drove, lights blazing in the darkness. The street was deserted save for the crowd gathered to watch a body being lifted onto a gurney.

It was still…lifeless.

He watched as the attendants began to lift the gurney with the body into the ambulance. The face was covered.

In his agitation, he nearly forgot to put the car into "Park" as he came to a screeching halt in the middle of the street. Two burly policemen attempted to stop him but he pushed them aside shouting, "My wife! My wife!" The cops stepped aside to let him through and he stood for a moment, trembling, afraid to view the face. He could see it was a woman. His heart was hammering in his ears. One of the ambulance attendants sympathized with his dilemma and gently uncovered the woman's face. Mike's relief was palpable and he nearly collapsed with the reprieve he'd been given. The driver of the ambulance was close by and supported Mike as he led him away from the tragedy. Someone else's family would be grieving this night, he thought, but thank God, not his – and for this notion, he felt guilt-ridden.

He drove home slowly. Sleep was probably not something he could hope for tonight, but if he didn't rest for at least a little while, he was going to be the one in the ambulance.

# # #

Sam arrived promptly at six a.m. and regarded the haggard figure who answered the door.

"I think I should drive, Mike. I don't think you're in any condition. What do you say we head on down to the precinct and do some digging? We can check on her cell phone activity for yesterday and see what calls came in or who she called. That might give us a clue as to what's going on.

"And Mike, I'm sure she's OK." Sam added, a bit too heartily.

Mike looked at Sam, but his gaze was unfocused. He did not agree. He knew something was wrong.

Sam kept to himself the fact that he'd had some friends of his checking for her car and credit card activity during the night. He was none too happy with the "sound of silence" either.

# # #

Exhausted, but jubilant, considering her circumstances, Jenny had broken free of the tie securing her right arm. She had no idea what the time was, but knew that she needed to work fast.

Having gathered all the strength she could muster, and after testing each tie for any weakness, she'd concentrated on freeing just one arm. Claire had secured her to a chair which had resilience – a flaw she had not considered. Jenny worked first on loosening the bond by pulling against it, and then by pushing as hard as she could into the cushion of the armchair. It had taken some time (about three hours, she would later discover) and several layers of skin, but it had worked. Once her hand was liberated, the rest was easy-peasy. Yup, that's it, easy-peasy. And Claire – I'm comin' for you!

Getting to her feet after having been bound in one position for so long, proved to be more difficult than Jenny thought. Thank God for yoga, she thought as she stretched out her body. She did a spinal lift first, but it was when she did a downward facing dog pose that she spotted the emergency box on the back wall of the theatre. It was also then that she realized that there was an urgency in her bladder she could no longer deny.

Luckily, Claire had thought of everything. Along with a popcorn machine, soda dispensers and a full complement of treats, there was a small restroom located behind the last row of seats to the right of the aisle. Jenny made a run for the restroom. She availed herself of a candy bar as she passed by on the way out, got a small bottle of water and headed for the emergency box which hung on the wall opposite from where she stood. As she passed the heavily padded double doors that led out of the theatre, she considered exiting, without having to face Claire. She also took into account the fact that, aside from most likely being locked, the doors might trigger an alarm, alerting Claire that Jenny was free. She didn't want Claire to know she was free until she was ready to face her and, Claire just might arrive armed

(oh yeah, armed and dangerous, that's our Claire.)

Jenny stifled a bray of laughter that threatened to escape. She feared that if she went down that road, there would be no return.

Upon inspection, the emergency box contained a fire extinguisher, a blanket, a small first-aid box, a mag flashlight, a length of rope and a fire escape mask.

Bingo!

Jenny hefted the extinguisher. She thought she could spray Claire in the face when she came into the theatre and surprise her the way she had surprised Jenny with the Pentathol.

The extinguisher was inoperable. OK.

She hefted the big mag light considering its weight. It still had batteries in it she discovered, but it too was inoperable. However, it would make a nice club. Actually, she thought, so would the extinguisher. She hid that between the third and fourth row of seats. The rope and the flashlight she brought to the seat where she had been tied.

If she was lucky, Claire wouldn't realize that Jenny was free until she came right up to her. Jenny would have the flashlight ready and swing. She could use the rope to tie Claire until she could get to a phone upstairs or until she could escape the grounds. If she wasn't so lucky, she could make a run for it and use the extinguisher as a club. Not as easy, but probably just as effective.

The video was still running.

Jenny gazed at herself and Claire in dismay.

Hindsight really *was* twenty-twenty!

# # #

Josh heard Sam's car pull up at six that morning. He'd slept badly that night, worrying about his mother and had been up since five a.m. He saw Sam go into his house and decided that whatever was happening, he needed to be there. Pulling on his clothes as fast as possible, he headed for the side door of Denise's house. Thinking better of it, he slipped into the kitchen and scribbled a note to Denise, letting her know that he'd gone with his father. Quietly, he tiptoed out and pulled the door shut behind him.

Josh got to his driveway as Sam and Mike were exiting the side door.

"Hey, Josh," Sam called. "What're you doin'? Shouldn't you be getting ready for school?"

"I'm not going." Josh replied. "I'm coming with you and dad."

"You should be in school, Josh," Mike began. "Denise…"

"I left a note. Told her I was going with you. I want to go, dad. Please…"

Mike looked at Sam who only shrugged.

"OK. Come on." Mike said. "But you have to listen and do as you're told. If we tell you to wait in the car…"

"I'll wait." Josh finished. "Thanks."

Josh climbed into the back seat of Sam's SUV and the three headed for the precinct.

# # #

"Yeah, that's it," Sam said reading from the printout that logged Jenny's calls the previous day. "The last incoming call she had was from Eberhardt Industries. That would be Claire Eberhardt and that came in at twelve twenty-six p.m. The last text message was to Josh at twelve thirty-four and that one, you already know. So…the last one to talk with Jenny was Claire Eberhardt. We tried calling the number, but no answer. I'm having a cruiser from the local precinct swing by just to see if Jenny's car is there."

"Hey, dad?   I think maybe I should tell you something."

After viewing the You Tube video on Josh's phone, Mike and Sam looked at each other and then both looked at Josh.

"I'm sorry, OK? I mean, she was so lousy to mom, I just wanted everyone to know what an asshole she was being."

"Don't say 'asshole'." Mike automatically corrected.

"You know, the kid could have something here." Sam said. "We don't know if she saw the video, but let's say she did. If she's got a temper, who knows how long she could let it simmer before she exploded. I mean, yeah, she's a big-shot, so we have to kind of tip-toe around, but we can still ask questions – like why she called Jenny yesterday and did Jenny say where she was headed."

"She kept telling me that there was something…that she didn't think that Claire was sincere, but I told her she was being foolish." Mike confessed. "Maybe she still is," he added. "Just because Claire was the last one to speak with her…"

Josh interjected.

"Dad. Tyler and his friends think she's a phony. Tyler says that if his dad wasn't killed, she would never have bothered to even say hello to his mom. He said that his mom and our mom are just charity cases to her. You know – she's nice to make herself look good."

"Josh, let me think…please." Mike said.

"Sorry." Josh mumbled.

Sam picked up his ringing phone, said a few words and tuned back to Mike.

"That was the police cruiser I asked to do a drive-by. They said they saw no cars at all – nothing in the driveway, anyway. Come on. We're going to go out there and ask Ms. Eberhardt just what the hell that conversation with Jenny was all about."

# # #

Claire awoke at seven-thirty a.m. after having had a wonderful night's sleep. She awoke thinking…there was something…and then a smile curved her lips. Of course. A wonderful present was waiting for her in the theatre and she couldn't wait to open it up! It would be a marvelous day for her…not so much for the present! She laughed aloud at her joke. "Not so much for the present…"

Claire laughed raucously, the sound echoing throughout the house.

It was a good omen…always good to begin the day on a high note!

Claire showered and dressed in old gardening jeans and a t-shirt. (She didn't want to soil any of her good garments after all.) She hummed as she made herself a delicious breakfast of an omelet with bacon, broccoli and goat cheese and a toasted croissant. She chose hazelnut coffee, put it into a "go cup" and headed downstairs. Perhaps she would be magnanimous and offer what's-her-name a sip of water…maybe. She unlocked the theatre doors and let them swing shut behind her.

Jenny lay as she had left her and the screen continued playing the video. The undulating color washed over her victim making her appear yellow, then blue, then green. She'd be green soon enough, Claire thought as she strolled over to where Jenny lay.

"Hey there, girlfriend," she called as she approached. "How're we doing this morning? Did you pee yourself yet? I expected it to stink of urine in here, but you must have held out. Too bad. It would have made you…"

Claire had reached Jenny's side. Her eyes widened in surprise as she realized that Jenny's ankles were not bound. She reached into her pocket just as Jenny swung the heavy mag lite directly into Claire's face.

# # #

Jenny stared at the expanding pool of blood in fascination. She couldn't tell whether it was coming from Claire's nose or mouth, but there were copious amounts of the stuff. In the constantly rippling light of the screen, it appeared black, then blue, then true red.

Shaking her head to bring herself back, she ran for the double doors of the theatre. They were locked. Claire must have the keys in her pocket, she thought.

Jenny headed back down the aisle to retrieve the keys. She reached the seat where she had been tied, and bent low with the intention of searching Claire.

Seeing the pool of blood, she was momentarily disoriented by the fact that there was no Claire.

Suddenly there was an inhuman cry and before she had a chance to turn, something wrapped around her neck, cutting off her air supply. Her hands flew up to her throat attempting to loosen whatever it was that was choking her. She felt the coarseness against her fingers and realized that it was the rope.

Jenny's weakened condition was no match for the demented Claire. Her last conscious thought was that she probably should have killed the bitch.

# # #

Mike, Sam and Josh stood at the gate of the Eberhardt estate. They had not had an answer from inside the house when they inquired at the locked gates.

"You'd think she'd have a staff, or something," Sam said. "Someone should be there."

Frustrated, Mike jammed his thumb against the bell.

"Can't we do something?" Mike asked.

"No." Sam said. "We need a search warrant to get in and we don't have probable cause. No judge is going to sign-off without that. Plus, she's an upstanding member of this community – at least as far as everyone is concerned. Claire's neither a suspect, a witness nor a person-of-interest. We have no leverage. We only wanted to talk and if she doesn't want to let us in, she doesn't have to."

"But she's the last one who…"

Mike never finished his sentence. His attention was drawn to the gate and he simply stared at his son who was smiling happily – from the other side.

"What the hell did you do?" Mike asked.

"Well, you guys couldn't get in, so I climbed the fence. I'm a kid. That's what we do!" Josh explained.

"All right kid. Since you're in, look for a box somewhere on that side of the fence. They've got to have something on that side to let themselves out – just in case the remote fails." Sam said.

Josh looked around and located the corresponding box. He opened the small door and pushed the button, allowing the gates to swing wide.

They piled back into Sam's truck and headed up the long driveway towards the mansion.

"Gates were open." Sam intoned. "She should get that checked."

Mike and Josh simply nodded in agreement.

# # #

Claire had hacked the rope that Jenny had extracted from the emergency fire box into several suitable lengths. She used it to tie Jenny back into the chair. When she finished, she went into the bathroom Jenny had used earlier and looked at herself in the oversized mirror. Blood was still streaming from her nose, but at least it wasn't gushing. She winced when she used a soft towel to mop the blood off her chin. Claire began to head for the elevator to take her to the second floor where she kept bandages and tape and small splints. She'd have to take care of herself for a bit before going into a hospital, where she would make up some story about falling down the stairs. First, however, she was planning on dosing out some of the same pain to her guest. Apparently, Jenny was coherent now. Claire began to think of just how much damage she could do to her before the end of the day.

She began entering the elevator, but thinking better of it, she went into the small workshop that was just outside the wine cellar. She found what she wanted and glanced around. Oh, she was going to have so much fun with all these goodies. There were hammers and pliers and electric drills and just so many things to play with.

Claire went back to the chair where she had Jenny tied down. She unrolled the duct tape and beginning at Jenny's ankles, bound her even more securely.

Don't think you'll get out of *this* quite so easily.

Lastly, Claire taped Jenny's forehead to the headrest of the chair. She did not tape Jenny's mouth.

She *so* loved the screaming.

"'Yes, little girl. You are mine. *All* mine. And you *will* scream."

Claire began to laugh but stopped as the pain washed over her.

She headed upstairs for an ice pack and bandages and a strong pain killer.

# # #

Mike and Sam instructed Josh to wait in the car while they went up to the front doors to knock.

"No doorbell?" Mike asked, looking at either side of the huge doors.

"Nah. Doorbell's only at the gate. Place like this…there's a butler or a maid to open the doors for you. These knockers here – they're really just for show.

"Betcha no one ever uses 'em." Sam added.

Mike tried anyway. They heard the knock echo hollowly inside the house.

Claire was in the upstairs bathroom when she heard it. The distinct boom of the knocker could be heard everywhere on the first and second floors.

She raced to her bedroom window and saw the green SUV at the top of the circular driveway. Who was that? It wasn't a staff member. How did they get past the gates? What the hell was she supposed to do now? If she answered the door, blood splattered all over her, there would be questions – from whoever it was. If she failed to answer the door, other consequences would arise.

Claire was working herself up into a panic.

The bleeding had mostly stopped. She quickly changed into a clean shirt and jeans, wincing as she automatically bent her head to button the jeans.

Inhaling deeply through her mouth, she took a bathroom towel and held it to her face, hiding her nose which had swollen to the size and color of a small eggplant and went down the stairs.

She'd deal with the intruder if it came to that.

# # #

"No, no. I'm fine." Claire said in answer to Sam's query. "There's always a lot of blood when you bang your nose hard enough. I don't believe it's broken, but when I went down the attic stairs, I slipped and hit the newel post and that's what did me in. So silly, I know.

"Anyway, what's going on about Jenny? Why, for heaven's sake, would you think that she'd be here?"

Sam referred to his notepad.

"A call came from this residence to Mrs. Palmer's – Jenny's phone at twelve twenty-six p.m. yesterday. That call lasted six minutes.

"Did you make that call, Claire?"

Claire nodded her head. "Yes."

"Would you mind telling us what that call was about?" Sam asked.

"No, of course not." Claire gestured for the men to sit as she pulled out an ottoman for herself. "I wanted to ask her if she was free this weekend for a barbeque. I'd planned on calling a few others, but got interrupted by my teapot's whistle. As I was having my tea, I remembered something I wanted to get that was in the attic. I...couldn't find it, came back downstairs and here I am."

Claire shifted the towel a bit and Sam caught the barest glimpse of her nose. It looked broken, not just bruised. He was no Doctor, but he had seen broken noses in his time, and this one fit the bill.

Mike asked, "Did Jenny say anything...anything at all to indicate where she was going?"

"Why no, Mike. She didn't say anything to me. She did mention, however, that she needed to get jeans or something of that nature. Have you checked out the mall or that small shopping district downtown? They have some lovely stores there. I know because my mother had half interest in one of them some time ago."

Sam sensed that they were going off track, and he didn't want to spend any more time chit-chatting about shopping. He stood.

"Do you think I could have a glass of water, Claire? I had one of those bacon, egg and cheese sandwiches and all the salt is getting to me. I'll get it, if you'd rather not move around too much."

"No, no, Sam. It's fine, although I probably will call my Doctor when you leave. He's one of the few who makes house-calls and I probably could use something for pain right about now." She grinned wryly as she rose and headed for her kitchen.

Ever the consummate hostess, she inquired, "Lemon?"

"Don't put yourself through any trouble, Claire." Sam replied.

"No problem." Claire answered.

Mike looked at Sam inquiringly and opened his mouth to speak.

Sam put his finger to his lips to quiet him.

"Josh is here." Sam said in a whisper.

"I know that." Mike said.

"No." Sam said, shaking his head. "He's *here*! As in: he was tip-toeing through the front hall just now. Claire had her back to him."

"Are you kidding me?" Mike said. "*Now* what do we do?"

"Follow my lead," Sam said. "And let's hope my 'gut instinct' is on target."

Claire came back with Sam's water. She smiled and made small talk with Mike while Sam drank, and offered her hopes that Jenny would be found soon.

"I will certainly call you if I hear anything," Claire said.

Both men thanked her for her time and her hospitality and left.

Once alone, Claire headed for the downstairs bathroom and selected two Percoset tablets from a small vial. She stared at the pills in her hand for a moment and shook out one more tablet, then washed the tablets down with water. Forgetting herself, she unceremoniously swiped her sleeve across her mouth and flinched.

Something else to make the bitch pay for, she thought.

She walked through the hall and rang for the elevator. When it arrived, doors opening with maddening slowness, she impatiently stabbed the down button.

She was not as alone as she thought.

Josh took note of Claire as she stepped into the elevator. The charming old-fashioned floor indicator above the doors marked her descent into the basement. He waited until the doors were closed and made a phone call as he fairly flew down the nearby stairs.

"Dad? Dad? It's me." Josh whispered. "I don't have much time. Please listen."

Sam had tumbled out of the car before Mike had gone out through the gates. Mike continued driving down the street in the exclusive neighborhood and put the police tag in the front windshield after he parked around a corner. He then proceeded to return to Claire's front gates at a dead run. Had Claire spotted him heading back towards the house, he'd have said that the car was suffering from mechanical difficulties.

Sam? Oh, he'd stayed with the car and, unfortunately, their cell phones had no signal. Could he use her phone, please?

It was a thin lie at best, but it would have to do.

Now, Mike took shelter behind the Leyland Cypress trees and he and Sam listened while Josh spoke.

"Gotta give it to your kid," Sam said to Mike. "If he leaves his cell phone on, we can hear everything that goes down. Of course, if Claire has nothing to do with Jenny's disappearance, we, well, really *you* are gonna have a little dancing around to do. If Claire really is innocent, and she does have her Doctor come in, then Josh can maybe get out of there while Claire is distracted. If she does see Josh or find him…well," Sam gave Mike a sidelong glance, "well," he continued, "we can worry about that when the time comes."

Mike was glad that Sam had stopped talking.

# # #

Josh watched Claire's movements from his position as he hid behind the bottom of the stairwell. He saw her march to the theatre doors and turn the bolt. She swung the door opened so hard that it banged against the wall behind it, leaving a dent where the handle punched through it. She'd been distractedly mumbling to herself since she'd walked off the elevator and as she stepped through the theatre's doors, she began bellowing.

Her ear-shattering screams were unintelligible, but Josh instinctively knew that it had to do with his mother.

Josh took a deep breath and ran, low and fast, aiming to get through the door before it swung shut. He just managed to slip through. The video he'd filmed was playing on the large screen in the front of the theatre washing the scene before him with slashes of color.

He stopped, momentarily mesmerized by the video. What he saw next made his stomach flip over.

It was his mom. She was tied to a theatre chair in a prone position and Claire was stalking down the aisle heading straight for her, a stream of profanity issuing from her. He wasn't even sure if his mom was alive.

He held his position as he searched about for a weapon. He saw nothing.

Josh was only fifteen years old, but physically took after his paternal grandfather – big-boned and broad-shouldered. He was already five feet, eleven inches tall and weighed about one hundred and ninety pounds. He was as solid as a brick and very fleet-footed. Much to his father's pride and his mother's dismay, he played offensive tackle on his school's football team.

Go Lions!

He attempted to determine whether it would be better to catch Claire as she was walking down the aisle or wait until she got to his mother's side. It took about five seconds for Claire to make that decision for him, as her long strides took her swiftly to her victim.

Her own ongoing diatribe and the blood rushing through her ears made it difficult for Claire to hear anything. She was literally seeing red and reached into her pocket as she reached Jenny's side. Claire pulled the Taser gun out as Josh caught her in a full-on tackle. The "oomph" sound she made when she went down gratified Josh, but his feeling of self-satisfaction didn't last because the next thing he felt was fifty-thousand volts coursing through his body. His limbs shook, his hair stood on end, his teeth chattered and his bladder let go.

# # #

Sam pulled his gun out of its holster and blew out the lock on the front door when he heard Claire's initial tirade.

Mike shot ahead, even as Sam was attempting to hold him back.

Sam did his best to keep Mike abreast of him. Thanks to Josh's open phone line, they had heard Claire screeching and a background noise they initially couldn't identify, until Mike snapped his fingers when he heard Jenny's voice.

"That's Maine," he said. "Remember Josh made the video…"

"The theatre!" Sam said.

They ran towards the stairs.

"Back off Mike. We don't know if she's armed." Sam warned.

"I don't care, Sam. That's my wife and my kid."

"Yeah, I got it. But you getting killed isn't gonna help. Stay behind me," Sam ordered.

Mike was angry but he took note of Sam's flat, cold eyes. Cop's eyes, he thought, and let him take the lead. He felt his heart thudding in his chest but he stayed behind Sam who ran low and led with his weapon.

The scene they encountered when they burst through the theatre doors turned Mike's blood to ice.

His wife was apparently unconscious and strapped down to a theatre chair and his son was on the floor and looked as if he was having a seizure. Claire was standing over Josh, grinning. Then Mike saw the Taser in Claire's hand.

"Drop it, Claire, or I'll drop you." Sam shouted – his gun aimed at Claire.

Mike had all but forgotten Sam's presence in his initial shock.

He watched as Claire's eyes widened and she licked her lips.

"I'm just defending myself, see?" Claire offered the hand that still held the Taser gun. "He's an intruder and he must have tied her up and I had to defend myself. He knocked me down and I had to defend myself didn't I? That's all it was. Self-defense…yes. Marvelous these little things are…" She looked quizzically at the Taser and then at Sam.

"Sam? What…" Claire took a deep breath and began to walk up the aisle towards Sam, the gun held limply down at her side.

"Sam. What a nice surprise. Can I offer you some tea? Perhaps, some delicious home-made cookies to go with the tea?"

Mike realized her bewilderment and nodded his head towards Sam. Sam nodded back and Mike slipped up behind her taking the Taser gun. Claire turned her head and saw him.

"Oh, Mike. You're here too? I know I said I'd get some tea and cookies – for both of you, of course, but I'm suddenly so very tired."

Sam took note of her unfocused eyes and drooping lids.

"Please, pardon my lapse in manners but I think I need to rest now and I need to get to a Doctor. The cameras are not kind, you see." She put her hands up to her face, gingerly touching her nose and sank into the nearest chair.

Once Mike had disarmed Claire, he raced down the aisle to check on his son and his wife, calling nine-one-one as he ran.

Sam, meanwhile took advantage of Claire's fugue state and cuffed her hands to the chair. She immediately closed her eyes and began to snore.

He too made a call asking that back-up be sent to Claire's residence, quickly explaining the situation.

"She's not going anywhere anytime soon." Sam said, indicating Claire. How are they? Do you need any help?" he asked.

"I think they'll be OK. Jenny is starting to come around and Josh is young and strong. I don't think a Taser will do him in. Besides, he'll be happy he has a great story to tell at school.

"You know, Sam. I've got a brave kid here." Mike said.

Sam nodded and smiled. "Yeah, you do, Mike. Hey, I'm going to go and make sure those gates are open for the ambulance. You just stay with them."

Sam turned to leave, but then turned back.

"Oh, hey, Mike? You guys want to go fishing this weekend?" He grinned.

Mike looked incredulously at Sam and then began to laugh.

THE END

THE HAND OF GOD

Detective Harry Ward hunkered down next to the body that had been impaled through the shoulder blades by the slender wooden cross. The seven-foot-high cross had hung more than thirty feet above the alter. Spotlights on either side illuminated the empty space where the cross had been suspended from the sanctuary's cathedral ceiling.

"How much do you think this thing weighs?" Ward asked.

His partner, Mark Delgado shrugged. "I dunno Harry. Could be forty, fifty pounds, maybe."

Harry Ward stood, squinted up towards the ceiling, calculating the distance.

"Hook's not broken on the cross itself." he observed walking carefully around the prostrate figure. "Gotta have given way up top. We need someone on a ladder or whatever will reach that high to go up there. Check to see if it was deliberately loosened. Don't know if he was the target or if it was one of the other priests. Although, when I talked to Father Mike – he's the one who found the body," he said by way of explanation to his partner. "He says he's never seen this priest before. I wonder if he could've been our perp."

"Dunno Harry. We'll run his prints when we get back. I just wanna know how the hell, 'scuse me…how the heck that thing came down and is standing up like that in his back. A knife I could understand…but this? It defies every law of gravity. The forensics guys took lots of pictures I hope? No one's gonna believe it, you know."

Ward nodded his head thoughtfully. "You got that right."

Four hours earlier…

Giancomo Lupo was running for his life, an incongruous broad smile on his face. He might be running for his life, but he had a plan. He always had a back-up plan.

He was usually able to do a job quickly and remove himself from the scene before anyone even knew he'd been there. This time had been very different. He'd managed to trap his quarry in a back ally behind McGregor's Bar and Grille. The job would have gone so much more smoothly had he been given his choice of weapons, but he had been restricted to a knife. His handler had been very clear on that fact. The clients wanted a clean slash across the target's throat. A message was being sent. Who the recipient of that message was, Lupo had neither the desire nor need to know.

If he was lucky, this recipient would ignore the message and he'd have another job. As it was, he was being paid handsomely for this job – one-half more than usual because the manner of the target's demise was being determined by the client.

The target, however, had not cooperated with Lupo's plan and had managed to dial nine-one-one for help as he ran. By the time Lupo had caught up with him, he could already hear sirens in the distance. No matter. He'd had a job to do and he, being the consummate professional, followed through. He had no concerns because he knew each block and hidey-hole in the neighborhood. That knowledge was part of his job.

Once, in a rare moment of introspection, Lupo had considered that his destiny had been pre-ordained. His last name, translated from the Italian language literally meant "Wolf" and that was what he was known as in his profession. He was a hunter who stalked his prey with much deliberation and caution and then moved in for the kill.

Lupo ran down Carroll Street and made a quick left, taking the small flight of stairs two-at-a-time. Opening the heavy wooden door at the top, he silently made his way into the church and crossed to the sacristy, entering a door on the right. He pulled off the blonde wig he'd donned for the occasion, removed the lifts from his pocket and thumbed through the garments contained in the wide drawers of the cabinet.

"OK, Father. I'm sure you won't mind if I borrow these for a short while," he muttered as he pulled the robe free.

Hastily, he pulled off the jacket that had been zipped up high on his neck, revealing a clerical collar and black shirt. Pulling off his sneakers, he stuffed the lifts into the heels of the black loafers he'd been carrying under his jacket and pulled the vestments over his head. Hastily, he jammed the wig, jacket and sneakers into a thin fabric bag that had also been under the jacket and stuffed it into a corner. He carefully finger-combed his own curly, dark brown hair. For the final touch, he perched a pair of wire-rimmed glasses on his broad nose and glanced into the small mirror that was hanging inside the closet door.

"Perfect," he declared softly and made his way back through the door from which he'd entered.

Taking a steadying breath, he bowed his head and sat in silence in the high-back, upholstered chair that was provided for priests during Sunday services. He was anticipating the arrival of the local police who would, of course, efficiently do a "door-to-door" search of the entire neighborhood in an effort to locate the perpetrator. Naturally, the "priest" now sitting and fingering his rosary beads would do his best to assist.

Lupo did not have long to wait.

Two uniformed officers entered through the main doors of the Church, respectfully removing their caps. Lupo counted to three and slowly lifted his head, his eyes questioning.

"Yes, my sons?"

"Father, we need to know if anyone has been in here, in the last ten to fifteen minutes."

"No...I...wait a moment...What would this person look like?"

"A man Father," one of the officers said. "About five foot eight or nine. Blonde hair, dark gray hoodie..."

Lupo managed a look of concern. "Actually, there was someone like that when I entered the sacristy. He was just coming through the doors you yourself used. He saw me and hesitated for a moment. I asked if I could help him. He shook his head and left."

Lupo stood to display his six-foot height. "I'm sorry, but that is all I can tell you."

As Lupo spoke, he made his way to the alter, his hands piously steepled together.

"That's OK Father. You've been a big help. Thanks."

"God bless you both," Lupo said earnestly, making the

priest's sign of the cross in the air in front of him.

The one officer who had spoken last, bowed his head briefly and made a grab for his phone as he exited with his partner. Lupo could hear him calling this new piece of information in.

Lupo bowed his head low to the alter, hiding his smirk of satisfaction. He began to rise when he heard a sound so loud it fairly vibrated his bones.

It was the last sound he was to hear on the earth.

The crack, pop and hiss of a well-developed fire were the next.

THE END

TRICK OR TREAT

The weather was perfect. It was the best day yet that October.

It was also the last day.

Katie and Nicky were upstairs getting ready for the evening's festivities, and Amy could hear them from the kitchen, arguing over who was going to carry the bigger of the two giant orange plastic pumpkins they would cart around while "trick or treating."

In the distance, Amy could hear the four o'clock whistle blow at Gantry Nuclear which was the source of revenue for almost all the townspeople in Shelby Downs, including her husband, Craig. He was the Environmental Controller of Research and Development who took his position very seriously but not much of anything else. His philosophy was that life was too short to spend it frowning, and he happily shared that thinking amongst everyone he knew. It made him a popular and respected man at work – and even more popular amongst his wife and children.

"Would you two please knock it off and get down here! If I hear any more yelling from up there, you two aren't going anywhere tonight!"

Amy was greeted by instant silence. She grinned to herself. At least they listened occasionally. She continued clearing the table from the evening's dinner, debating whether she should bother saving the leftovers. The probability was that once they were placed in the refrigerator as leftovers, they would exit as some exotic form of fungi and be tossed anyway. Amy hated having to throw food away. Her mother's admonition about the starving children in China always popped to the forefront of her mind whenever she faced the decision of refrigerate or dump. She smiled.

OK, small creatures! It's party time! She scraped all the leftovers onto one plate and slid open the glass door leading onto their spacious redwood deck. She loved this deck. It had taken Craig six weeks last summer to complete his project. He had measured, leveled, fitted every piece of wood and driven every screw – all without ever having so much as built a bookcase before. He was so proud of it when he finished, he was fairly preening. He denied this of course, but she knew.

The back of their home faced undeveloped woods, and one-half mile beyond that, wetlands. It was perfect and private. They'd had countless birthday parties, holiday parties and barbeques here even before the deck and still, the best times she and Craig had out here had been after the children had gone up to bed and they were alone. They would sit on warm summer nights and even on cool fall evenings with their little wood burning stove glowing cheerily, as they cuddled together under a canopy of stars.

They had purchased a big squishy outdoor chaise lounge for these occasions, and they'd curl up, wrapped snugly in blankets listening to the crickets and all the other night sounds and tell each other their hopes, their dreams, their fears. They knew each other's deepest secrets and, with that, came a sense of peace and oneness.

Amy sighed blissfully as she walked to the furthest end of the deck and tossed the leftovers.

"Eat, drink and be merry little creatures, for tomorrow…" She left the sentence unfinished and shivered a bit as she made her way back into her cozy kitchen. It's really getting chilly out there, she thought, rubbing her hands together. Real fall weather! Maybe we'll get some wood into that fireplace tonight and roast some marshmallows when we get back. Just thinking about that made her warmer.

Five minutes later, Katie and Nicky pounded down the stairs all decked out in their Halloween finest. Nicky was a Ninja Turtle tonight. He was still faithful to his all-time favorite characters, despite all the intervening fads. He was momentarily engaged with practicing his best karate moves while trying desperately to keep his balance. His four-year-old body was sturdy and still carried a bit of baby fat, however, and those sleek moves didn't come easily. His brows were furrowed in concentration and Amy found herself grinning inwardly. He looked so much like Craig when his little face took on that look of determination.

Katie, on the other hand, was very much a lady and wore her "beautiful witch" costume with aplomb. Even at six, you could see the delicate beauty she would be as she grew into womanhood. Her high cheekbones, creamy white skin and full mouth were a gift from her mother, but she'd inherited her father's black hair and vivid blue eyes – the antithesis of her blonde mother.   He liked to call her his "little Snow White" and she'd roll her eyes in mock despair and complain, "Oh, Daddy!" Of course, they all knew she absolutely reveled in the glow of her father's attention.

The doorbell rang with urgency and Katie ran to answer it. She knew it was the group of kids with whom they would tour Main Street this evening. She opened the door and a variety of tiny creatures tumbled into the hallway. There were clowns, robots, ghosts, two black cats, Superman, a ballerina, and even a giant hamburger on a bun, resplendent with onions and cheese.

Squeals of excitement rang throughout the house and Amy dutifully admired each and every child. She quickly lined everyone up for pictures and then waved to the two harried mothers who had finally managed to make their way through the door. Greetings were shouted over the din.

Cassie was busy counting noses and looked around. "There's a unicorn missing!"

Amy looked around the group and noticed a four-year-old unicorn sucking its thumb, halfway hidden by the open door, behind Elisabeth.

Cassie turned as Elisabeth pointed behind her.

"Oh, there you are, Pamela! Do try and keep up with the rest of the crowd, my dear. We don't want any unicorns on the loose tonight, do we?"

She smiled encouragingly as she coaxed the child in with a gentle hand. Elisabeth was fairly new to the neighborhood. She and her husband George had moved to Shelby Downs from London, when her husband was made a Vice President at Gantry. Amy had liked her immediately when they'd met at mutual friends Memorial Day barbeque in May. She thought that Elisabeth was like a breath of fresh air in their sleepy little town. In a short time, she'd brought a lot of new ideas into the local pre-school's summer program and always seemed to attract attention with her wit and her charming accent.

Cassie agreed with Amy's appraisal of Elisabeth. Cassie and Amy had been friends since kindergarten and suffered through schools, boyfriends, weddings and babies together, and by this time, were capable of practically reading each other's thoughts. Even before she introduced the two, Amy had known Cassie would be as fond of Elisabeth as she herself was.

Amy gave last minute instructions to her two little ones about staying together, grabbed her jacket and purse and joined the clamor of everyone piling back out the door.

Amy was going to meet Craig at the other end of town because he'd had to stay late at the office tonight, and he thought it would be fun to join her and the others on the second half of their trick or treat route. She congratulated herself in a modest way whenever she thought of her life – her husband, her children, her home. She had to admit to herself – she had it made. She'd married the tall, dark, handsome love of her life, had her two beautiful children, and was living an ideal life in small town America where crime rates were low and community spirit ran high.

She brought herself back to the present with a jolt when her foot caught on a tree stump hidden by the leaves underfoot. Cassie caught her arm to steady her and Amy giggled in embarrassment. "That's what I get for daydreaming! Next time, I'll probably land flat on my face!"

The sun was dropping rapidly as it always did at this time of year. The kids took advantage of the deepening darkness and began turning on their flashlights. All the mothers had agreed that it was a good idea for each child to carry one to guide their way in the darkness, but of course, the flashlights were targeted at everything but the ground. The lights were dancing crazily off the surrounding houses and trees, making them appear to be waving their limbs wildly into the night.

Cassie was doing her fifth nose count in as many minutes and called loudly to Amy.

"Hey! Am I crazy, or have I lost my ability to count beyond thirteen? Come over here and help me!"

Amy glanced quickly around seeking Katie and Nicky. She spotted them as they strolled passed the front of the old Grover house, casually swinging their pumpkins. She called to the children to wait up for a minute and hurried over to Cassie.

"We're supposed to be trailing after fifteen kids and I keep counting thirteen. I think these darn flashlights are throwing me off!" Cassie laughed.

Amy had been counting while walking towards Cassie and was puzzled to discover she only counted thirteen also.

"Cassie! Where's Elisabeth?" Amy asked.

"Whaddya mean, 'where's Elisabeth'? She was right behind me two minutes ago. Elisabeth! Yo, Elisabeth!"

Cassie's voice carried loudly, and a few of the children milling close by glanced up questioningly. "She's probably off with the missing two talking to someone. You know her!"

Amy sighed. "I know. Someone asks for directions, and she feels compelled to walk them to their destination."

Cassie howled uproariously. She was Amy's best friend, and probably the most boisterous person Amy knew – which was probably why they had always been best friends, Amy thought. They were the perfect foil for each other's personalities. The two locked arms and herded their charges ahead of them as they scuffled through the leaves that decorated the sidewalks and gutters of Main Street. Choruses of "trick or treat" were being rattled off as doors opened to reveal eager faces, and precious candies were dropped into open bags.

The darkness was settling in heavily now, and were it not for the dancing flashlights, it would have been impossible to see anything due to the dense awning of trees overhead. Hushed voices and nervous titters could be heard as the group passed the small cemetery at the end of town.

The low, wrought iron gate in front stood guard either for those outside or perhaps in, and the blue-white light of the half-moon reflected dully off the headstones. Toilet tissue streamers, leftovers from mischief night, floated lazily in the light breeze blowing in from the east, and a vague aroma of cat urine drifted along, making noses wrinkle.

"Ugh! Gross!" Amy remarked, wrinkling her nose in disgust.

"Craig says they're looking to change the chemical they use for a sealant, 'cause so many people on this end of town are starting to complain about that stench, but so far…"

Amy's words were cut off by excited cries from the children at the forefront of the group. She and Cassie glanced quickly at each other and headed in the direction of the commotion.

Nicky was stomping his feet in excitement and confusion and chattering madly to both his sister and his best friend, Michael.

He looked up as his mother approached. His eyes were wide with surprise.

"Mommy, over there! Jackie and Lisa and Sandi…over there! I saw them…they fell in! Over there, Mommy!"

He was pointing his stubby index finger toward a huge pile of leaves that were mounded at the base of the ancient oak tree in the northeast corner of the cemetery. The tree looked ominous in the moonlight; gnarled and black and forbidding.

Amy shook her head. "Calm down there, buddy. You don't fall into a pile leaves and go under. The leaves aren't a lake!"

"But Mommy, I saw them! I saw them!" Nicky insisted.

"OK! OK! We'll just check it out, sweetie. You wait here."

Amy thought fleetingly of how much less frightening things looked in the bright sunshine and fervently wished those were the conditions right now. She called to Cassie to watch the others and jogged in the direction of Nicky's still pointing finger, shaking her head in exasperation. She reached the mound and swore mildly as she felt her foot catch, once again, on the raised stump of a tree and quickly spread her arms out to give herself balance. She thrashed her way through the leaves, scattering them widely. Someone's gonna be really ticked off at me when they have to rake these up again tomorrow, she thought wryly. She'd tromped through the entire mound and found nothing when she realized she'd lost her sneaker.

"Damn! How the hell did I manage this?" she muttered under her breath. She attempted to re-trace her steps and realized it was useless. The flashlight she was using gave off only a small circle of light and finding a black sneaker in all that blackness was just about impossible.

Her light hit upon something shining as she was waving it around, and she headed towards it for closer examination.

It was her sneaker…or something extremely similar. She couldn't quite tell, since it was covered in a substance resembling honey, but smelling suspiciously like a kitty litter box desperately in need of a change. She instinctively pulled back when the odor reached her. She hesitated reaching for the shoe, hating to lose a nearly brand new, seventy-dollar pair. Her hand reached out haltingly and she heard Cassie call to her. She shuddered at the horrific odor and pulled her hand back. She couldn't do it. Sticking her hand into that foul smelling goo would make her barf, she thought. She decided to talk to Craig when she saw him tonight and tell him just how bad it really was around here. The stench was permeating everything. Something was going on. Something was not right at all.

Amy quickly stepped out, doing a little half-step on one socked foot towards the waiting group. They had huddled very close together – probably more for solace than from cold, Amy thought. She realized how sensitive children were to the moods of the adults around them, and right now these kids were sensing worry and confusion in the adults they trusted.

"I'm sorry. I know you were only gone for a minute or two, but I...Why are you hopping on one foot Amy? What happened to your shoe? Did you find anything? We seem to be missing a few noses around here..."

Amy caught the tremor in Cassie's breathless voice as she delivered this news in one quick rush of words. She took a deep breath to steady her own.

"No...nothing. Who's, uh...missing?"

"Jackie, Lisa, Sandi," Cassie replied, the tremor in her voice even more pronounced. "The Williamson's bunch. The kids said that the girls ran up ahead of everyone and started jumping in the pile of leaves. Jackie cried out but she was half-buried and Lisa and Sandi – they started heading in her direction and Lisa fell and Sandi went to help her and she went down too and then the three of them started flailing around and the little ones started panicking and no one knows what happened after that.

"Michael said they disappeared under the leaves. Some of the kids said that Nicky said the leaves swallowed them. Gina said they're hiding in the cemetery to scare everyone."

Amy glanced down at Nicky, who had sidled closer to his mother.

"OK, Cass. Let's not over-react. Are all the others here?"

"Yeah. Everyone besides the original two and Elisabeth and now these three – that makes five kids, one adult. So I guess that's OK 'cause they must be with her. At least I guess they are..." Her voice trailed off.

"All right, all right. Let's just think here for a minute. The ground didn't open up and swallow them Cass. There's a reasonable explanation. We just don't know what that reasonable explanation is yet, exactly." Amy said cautiously. "But for now, let's just start by calling them and then we'll move on past the cemetery and get ourselves to Phil's Gas Station. That's where we're supposed to meet Craig and I'm sure we can get this whole thing straightened out.

"There are no houses here, so the probability that they went into someone's home is practically nil. And, if it's actually necessary, there's the police station right across Middletown Road – which I'm sure we won't need." Amy added hastily when she saw the look of panic that crossed Cassie's face.

They all called loudly for the missing three, with warnings of dire consequences if they didn't reveal themselves in a timely manner. The group hung together quietly, their ebullient moods deflated. Prompted by Amy and Cassie, they began to shuffle together past the cemetery and toward Phil's. Both mothers kept their arms spread wide in a sort of parody of a shepherd protecting his flock. They kept up an ongoing chatter, as much for themselves as for the children, in order to keep at bay the thoughts which kept bubbling up to the surface of each of their minds – thoughts of havoc and foul play and unpleasant things that go bump in the night.

They arrived at the gas station a few minutes later and Amy searched about for the familiar face of her husband. She spotted him an instant later, lounging against a light pole, reading the Shelby Register. He looked up when he heard footsteps approaching, but his welcoming grin quickly faded when he saw Amy's strained face.

Amy could feel her heart slip back into her chest as it fell from her throat where it had been clinging since she started searching through the leaves. She ran to Craig and hugging him briefly, quickly bringing him up to speed on what had been happening. Craig looked down at Amy's shoeless foot and shook his head.

Cassie ushered the children around them.

"Listen, just relax, you two. We'll retrace your route and I'm sure we'll find them hiding somewhere. They probably think they're pulling off the joke of the century on you guys."

Listening to Craig's words made things seem so reasonable.

"Sure. That's it!" Amy said.   Cassie nodded in agreement. "Those kids have been plotting this for weeks now, I'll bet. They're probably off somewhere having a big ha-ha over making us run around through leaves, yelling like ninnies. But, let me tell you, someone is going to get it for making me lose my sneaker in that muck!"

Amy slipped her hand into Craig's and motioned Cassie over for a quick conference. The group of children who, only a short while ago had been loud and full of Halloween spirit now stood quietly, feet shuffling uneasily as they awaited direction from the adults.

"OK kids! We're going to go back the way we came for a bit and find those little jokers." Craig said smiling brightly to the surrounding group of small, solemn faces. "We'll go up the rest of the way to Main Street together, and I *mean* together," he added a bit more sternly.

Or to Middletown Road and the police station Amy thought uneasily to herself. The children quietly gathered together and started walking back towards the cemetery. Katie slipped her hand into her father's free one as they started walking.

"Hey kids, I have an idea. Let's all of us try calling for Jackie, Lisa and Sandi and see who can call the loudest." Craig said.

Small voices began tentatively calling the missing three children, and grew louder as they kept walking.

"Good idea, Craig. At least it gives them something to do to take their minds off things," Cassie offered.

Amy's mind was in turmoil as they walked. What would she say to the parents of these children? How could she explain to them that their three children just "disappeared" while they were out trick or treating!

Craig and Amy led the small party through the night, each with their own thoughts, while Cassie brought up in the rear.

They had walked for about three or four minutes when the screaming started.

And what happened from that moment on would not be told the same way by any two people.

Amy and Craig were startled out of deep thought when they heard the piercing cry. Part of Amy's mind was thinking that it couldn't be human because no one could scream that loud or that long. It had to be some sort of animal or a recording...

It seemed to take forever, the way things do in a dream, to turn in the direction of the sound. Amy saw Cassie, who seemed to be kneeling in worship at a tree, and a small clown appeared to be playing peek-a-boo at her side with only his head and shoulders visible.

Amy began urgently gathering the other children about her in a small, protective knot with her own two already clinging to the edges of her jacket. Craig sprinted across the few feet of space between him and Cassie and reached down for the small clown head which had now disappeared under the leaves. At once, he realized he was in trouble. He felt the tremendous power of the muck which grabbed hold of his lowered arm. The overpowering stench of cat urine permeated his nostrils as he fought to free himself.

Amy watched in horror as Cassie was violently jerked flat out on her left side. Her left arm was twisted cruelly behind her back, her right hand opening and closing spasmodically. Craig, meanwhile, was having his own problems. His breathing was labored because of the ammonia fumes and it now seemed that one arm which was held fast in the slimy mire was numb below his elbow. Part of his brain noted – almost with detachment – that the pile of leaves seemed to be taking on a life of their own.

Cassie's free right arm could be seen jerking wildly now, almost as if she were merrily waving good-bye to some unseen group of friends in the distance. She had stopped screaming.

Amy stood watching the scene in dazed shock, her brain refusing to register and accept what she was seeing.

Finally, the cries of her young charges reached her consciousness and she was moved into action.

She whipped around to warn the children to stay close to each other – a totally unnecessary warning since they were already glued together – when she felt the ground begin to shift.

Earthquake!

"Oh God! It's an earthquake! That's it!"

Her cry rang of relief as her mind hurtled to embrace an acceptable reality. But, even as this truth fought to assert itself within her, her eyes were telling her that her worst nightmare had only just begun.

A small Ninja had been pushed to the outside of the huddling group of confused, whimpering children. Looking down, he'd discovered that his pumpkin, which was filled with trick or treat loot was no longer on his arm, but had landed on its side near a small tree a few feet away. His four-year-old mind fought to make a decision to stay on the perimeter of the group or to run and retrieve his once-a-year booty.

It hadn't looked so scary. It was, after all, his very own pumpkin filled with the goodies he'd collected. And, after he went home that night, his mom and dad would look through all his goodies "just to make sure" – sure of what he wasn't exactly clear on – but in the end, he'd be able to select a few pieces of candy each afternoon, sit on the porch in his favorite rocking chair and savor just how really sweet life was.

As he reached to pick up his plastic orange pumpkin, his expression became one of astonishment. The pumpkin seemed to be coming to life. It tilted, righted itself, and was now grinning madly, an eerie yellow-orange glow emanating from its depths and a glob of something shiny drooling from its left eye. Nicky tried to get closer, but was pushed back by the horrible stink coming from the thing.

"Nickeeee…"

The scream was coming from behind him, and as he whirled around, the ground began to shift beneath his feet. He tried to take a step, but discovered that his shoes must have been nailed into the ground, because his feet just wouldn't move. Nicky looked down and was amazed to discover he was up to his ankles in the same stuff that his pumpkin was now vomiting.

Amy was running towards her son even before she realized she'd taken a step. The sounds of screaming and sobbing children seemed to engulf her and she struggled to retain her rapidly thinning thread of sanity.

She reached Nicky in a fraction of a second, but not before he was jerked to his knees. She lunged forward to grab his outstretched arms.

"Mommy, mommy, help me! I can't get up!"

A bubble of hysteria began to rise within her and she fought to keep herself from laughing insanely as a part of her brain, replayed an ancient TV commercial in her head, "Help me. I've fallen and I can't get up…"

She had hold of his wrists now and braced her feet. But her shoeless foot would not maintain a grip on the slimy earth and she felt herself slip-sliding even as she saw her son's chubby little thighs disappear beneath the reeking pile of leaves.

"Mommy, it hurrrts…"

Craig was in awe of the strength which was holding him fast. He lifted his face up towards the sky in an effort to find fresh air to gulp into his straining lungs. A string of profanities, such as he hadn't used since his early youth, poured out from him. He was buried almost up to his midriff now, and leverage was nearly impossible. He could hear screaming in the distance, but was too engrossed in his own struggles to tune it in. He had lost his struggle to maintain a hold on the little clown who had long since sunk into the depths of the leaves. Now, he saw Cassie's head disappear beneath the surface of the leaves and somewhere in his head was the thought that he'd have to be the one to tell her husband, Christopher, that his wife had apparently been consumed by a pile of autumn leaves.

Suddenly, his left arm, which had been flailing wildly for a grip, found one. Splinters gouged themselves into his hand as he took hold of a broken limb. He concentrated all of his considerable strength and took a deep breath.

He found himself vaguely thinking about all those mornings of bench pressing, as his left arm strained to lift his body weight and free him from the stuff that had taken a strangle hold of his arm and was rapidly ascending up the right side of his body.

With an effort that expelled the air from his lungs and forced a tight grunt from his compressed lips, he began to pull himself up.

Amy's grip on Nicky tightened as she felt herself sliding towards him. His voice had become very small and whispery now as the full reality of his predicament fell upon him. She dully heard Katie's voice in the background alternately screaming for her and for her brother.

"Stay back, Katie! Stay back!"

Amy's voice broke into a sob now as she realized the futility of her effort. The honey colored, foul smelling sludge was winning its fight to capture her son and had now decided to enwrap her as well in its death grip. Her white sock, which had looked absurd next to her black sneaker, had disappeared and the bottoms of her jeans were now covered with the amber gel and gaily decorated with red, orange and yellow leaves.

Suddenly, she felt strong arms wrapped around her middle pulling hard. She felt Craig's strength and the scent of him over-rode the ammonia stench. She felt as if she'd been jerked back from the brink of a terrifying precipice and redoubled her efforts at pulling out her son.

"No, Amy, let go. It's OK. Just let go!"

Craig's voice was gentle and totally inappropriate for the moment, she thought, and there's no way I'm letting go.

"C'mon, babe. Let go. Let go. It's all right."

"Craig, are you crazy?" Amy's voice was a hoarse whisper fighting to be heard. "I can't. I won't. Help me, Craig! Please, help me pull!"

Amy felt her voice weakening as she fought to maintain her grip. Then, suddenly, it all slipped away.

"C'mon, Amy. C'mon. It's OK. Let go, will ya?"

The dim, orange light permeating her consciousness as she opened her eyes at first confused her, but then told her it was early morning. Craig's arms were around her waist, holding her tight against him. Amy, in turn, had a death grip on the pewter rung of their headboard. She was drenched in sweat and her heart was beating like a trip hammer.

She slowly peeled her cramped fingers off the rung and smiled wryly at their stiffness. She frowned as the dream came rushing back at her – the same dream which had been haunting her sleep now for almost a week. She slipped around until she was face to face with her husband.

"The same dream, right?"

"Yup. The same damned one – over and over and over."

Craig grinned. "That's probably 'cause I've been putting off raking that mess in the backyard for over two weeks now. I wouldn't be surprised if someone did get swallowed up out there!"

He tickled her gently and she giggled. If you analyze this dream, she thought, I bet it means I'm just afraid of losing my near-perfect life. And, when it came down to it, this was the perfect moment in that perfect life. They kissed slowly at first, and then with increasing urgency.

"Mommy! Mommy! Tell Katie I have to go." Little fists banged on the door with surprising strength. "She's in the bathroom and won't get out! Mommy!"

The loud insistent voice was calling from behind their closed bedroom door, breaking the mood of the moment.

They grinned at each other. Oh, well! That's my perfect life, Amy thought, amused.

Amy kissed Craig lightly on the lips before slipping out of bed to let Nicky into their bathroom. She glanced out the window as she slipped into her robe.

The weather was perfect. It was the best day yet that October.

It was also the last day.

THE END

ONE OF THE ORIGINAL SHORT STORIES YOU

WILL FIND IN VOLUME TWO...

TURN THE PAGE FOR AN EXCERPT...

UNDERWEAR ISLAND

She watched as her spirit drifted lazily by on the sun-sequined water, which was odd as she herself was floating face down.

The day had started well enough. She and her friends were taking the catamaran out to the other side of Underwear Island and having a picnic lunch there. This would typically be followed by a little "playing around" between the two sexes and eventually, the twenty-minute sail back to the mainland. At least, that had been the plan as told to her by her summertime boyfriend, Jason. However, something had gone terribly wrong.

When the group had arrived, they noticed a small canoe pulled up onto the tiny beach that graced the northern end of the island. This was not terribly unusual. It might perhaps impinge on their privacy for they could not enjoy their picnic or their usual frolic through the jungle-like growth of the island. It was then that they would fling their clothing about as they ran, much like Hansel and Gretel tossing crumbs behind them as they went through their own woods. The romp would end on the north-western end of the island where each would slip off their underwear, spiking it on the branch of one of the old laurel leaf willow trees there. Each of the old, dead trees was festooned with underwear in various stages of decomposition – a testament to the many years the island had served as a hangout for the generations of kids who vacationed on the mainland.

Lunch had gone pretty much as usual when the guys, headed up by Marc, began a food fight starting with the pickles, followed by the coleslaw and the cupcakes that had been meant for dessert. The icing now gaily decorated nearby rocks, wild grass and the girls.

It began when Sara's best friend Wendy ran off over the dune towards the ocean. She had been the target of most of the rations and was faring none too well under the burden of the coleslaw which clung tenaciously to the cupcake icing. She'd wanted nothing more than to jump into the water and rinse off the sticky combination. It was fifteen minutes before her sometimes boyfriend, Carl, realized that she hadn't returned.

Carl climbed to the top of the dune, looked out for a moment towards the ocean, turned and raced back down the dune so fast he lost his footing and tumbled the rest of the way onto the sand, landing face down.

The rest of the kids (there were six to start with) began laughing at his antics. Carl was well known as the group's undisputed clown after all. However, when he lifted his face to them, they saw the look of terror on his sheet-white face.

"Where's Wendy?" Marc asked, as yet only mildly concerned.

Carl gulped, his Adams apple bobbing mightily.

"She's…there…there…she's…" he stammered, pointing a shaky finger back over the dune. Carl swallowed hard, trying to gain control over his speech. He'd been trying to get to his feet, and now sat back down hard.

"She's what, man? Naked? Dead?" Mark laughed nervously.

"B…B…Both" was all that Carl could manage.

"Aw, fuckin' A…" Marc muttered as he trudged over to the dune. "What the hell is your problem?"

It took Marc about ten seconds to see what Carl's

quandary was once he reached the top of the dune. His problem was lying naked on the wet sand, legs akimbo, feet being tickled by the incoming tide, cell phone in her outstretched right arm, as if she were attempting to keep it dry. But there was so much blood…blood that had soaked into the wet sand…blood that turned the water swirling around her feet into a pink froth. Marc's belly protested and he dry-heaved.

The remaining five now sat in a semi-circle, backs against an outcropping of rocks that protruded from the sand, well away from what was left of Wendy.

They had ascertained that her cut throat, having been sliced almost from ear to ear, had probably been the cause of her demise. This they'd discovered when the girls demanded that the boys pull her out of the incoming tide, lest she be washed out to sea. The boys had lifted her, two taking one arm each and one holding her by her ankles, when her head had lolled, revealing most of the inner workings of her neck.

Mark gagged forcefully, Jason, who was Sara's date, screamed and Carl's eyes rolled back in his head and he folded onto the sand. Sara and Jessica, who had been watching to see that Wendy's body was handled respectfully given her lack of attire, screamed in unison, unconsciously clutching their throats as they retreated down off the dune upon which they had been watching the three boys. They were no longer concerned about Wendy's nudity; they were now profoundly aware of their own vulnerability.

Jason was the next to go missing......

AUTHOR BIO

While growing up as an only child in Brooklyn, New York, F.X. MANDICH would make up stories for her own amusement.

"Daydreaming got me through wait-time at doctor's offices, supermarkets and airports. The only people unhappy with this tendency were my parents!"

Once she decided to journal her daydreams, she contributed stories to her high-school magazine and was one of several editors of her school newspaper.

While working her way through college, she believes she wrote the only non-fiction she's ever penned – press releases for a large advertising firm's public relations department.

She stopped working, got married and two children later, moved to a small town on the East Coast where she had some of her short stories published.

If you are a fan of the creepy-crawly, things-that-go-bump-in-the-night, or just like the unusual, you're in the right place.

Happy Reading!